WARNING

This book contains sexually explicit scenes and adult language. It may be considered offensive to some readers. This book is for sale to adults ONLY.

* * * * * * * * * * * * * * * * * * *

Please store your files wisely where they cannot be accessed by underage readers.

Other books by Shyla Starr:

Tenacious Billionaire BWWM Romance Series

Adalia is too proud to accept help from the billionaire playboy, Trent Dawson. How long can she maintain her resolve? The bank is at her heels to repossess her business. To make matters worse, Adalia finds suspicious evidence of Trent's philandering ways. She must determine whether to trust Trent with the fate of her business and her heart.

Elusive Billionaire Romance Series

Billionaire Hendrick is trying to repair his company's image by putting in some volunteer work, building a school and hospital for the impoverished children in Africa. There, he meets a beautiful African American volunteer, Jocelyn. They hit it off right away but does she belong in his world?

Lonely Billionaire Romance Series

Tricia was hired to care for billionaire John's wife, who is dying. An unlikely romance emerges after his wife, Rebecca, gives John permission to pursue his happiness after she is gone.

Ardent Billionaire Romance Series

Deirdre doesn't know what to make of the gorgeous man that seems to be interested in her. His name is Parker Walters and he seems friendly enough. There is just something off about him. Why is he trying the hide the fact that he is the heir to his father's billion dollar software empire?

Fervent Billionaire BWWM Romance Series

Alexandra had never been with a white man before. She had seen William at the café before but she always kept her distance. It was unfortunate that their first chance meeting happened when she dropped her breakfast and spilled coffee all over his expensive business suit.

Audacious Billionaire BWWM Romance Series

Chante is torn between staying close to a man beyond her league, and fleeing from him to spare herself from a hopeless position. But she finds she is propelled into a place where she needs to confront her doubts and cast her fate aside to follow the dictates of her heart. Damned if she does and miserable is she doesn't, how will Chante face the events that will lead her to a place of pure happiness or to the pits of a broken heart?

Get the latest update on new releases from the author at:

https://shylastarr.com/newsletter/

This book is Part Three of the "Persuasive Billionaire BWWM Romance Series"

1 - Love Invested

Stacey is trying to keep a handle on her life the best that she can. She is on the verge of losing her job and her apartment, while taking care of her sick grandmother. Her life takes an unexpected turn when she meets Charlie, who works for the construction company that is attempting to persuade her to move out of her home.

2 - Love Divested

After discovering that Charlie has a fiancée, Stacey's world has turned upside down. She cannot help but feel as if she is in over her head. Struggling with her job, her bills and her family, will Stacey be able to figure out how she can get her life straightened out?

3 - Love Reinstated

Stacey decides that she has to put Charlie behind her and move on with her life. As Stacey dates Tony and is pulled into his world, she slowly realizes that although she likes him, it might not be enough to brush aside her feelings for Charlie. Leaving everything behind, she lets herself get lost in the money and privacy that Tony brings to her.

4 - Love Confirmed

Stacey can't believe the turn of events in her life. After losing her grandmother and running away to Tony's private island, she was content to stick her head in the sand and forget her past. But a proposal from Charlie changes everything.

5 - Love Divine

Stacey must ensure she relaxes in order to keep her baby safe. But life is never that easy. Her new husband's father is bent on sabotaging their fledgling investment firm. To make things worse, her brother-in-law isn't content with just being in the background. Stacey finds herself wishing she could have the brothers patch things up.

Persuasive Billionaire BWWM Romance Series

Love Reinstated

Book Three

By Shyla Starr

Copyright Revelry Publishing 2018

Table of Contents

Chapter One

THE NEXT few seconds seemed to be a complete blur. As soon as Stacey saw Adele's lips on Charlie, she had turned around blindly and left the room. She had to get out of there right that instant. The last thing she wanted to do was cry. There was no point in crying; she had broken up with Charlie. If he wanted to finally fool around with Adele, then let him.

Allison said something, but Stacey didn't hear it. She was practically jogging down the hallway to the staircase. Allison was hot on her heels. Stacey didn't want to turn around and see if Charlie had followed her or not.

Down the stairs she went. She spilled out into the party and started weaving through the crowd. She was halfway to the entrance when someone grabbed her arm. Startled, she let out a cry and turned around.

It was Tony. It took Stacey a couple of seconds to remember that she had come to the party with him.

"There you are!"

"Uh, yeah, here I am," she mumbled and scanned the crowd for Charlie.

"Listen, come with me to the patio. There is –"

"I can't. I'm sorry." She shook her head. "I have to go. I have a massive headache and I'm in a lot of pain."

Concern flickered across his face, along with something else that Stacey couldn't put her finger on. Tony let go of her. Someone bumped into her as they walked by. The party seemed to have doubled in size in the short time Stacey had been upstairs.

"Thanks for inviting me," she said quickly.

"Wait, how are you getting home?" Tony called after her as she left.

"I'll call a cab!"

She pushed her way through the crowd and out of the front door. Even here the crowd was thick. Her frantic state was starting to mix with feelings of claustrophobia from the mass of bodies surrounding her on all sides. She was on the verge of either passing out or bursting into tears if she didn't get out of this place quickly.

Stacey took off down the driveway toward the gate. Tears were pressing against her eyes. She cursed herself for acting so stupidly. How could she be so upset? She had opted out of dealing with Charlie and his family drama. She had no right to be so upset.

"There you are!"

Stacey froze for a second. But it was enough for Charlie to grab her arm exactly where Tony had. He turned her around. Her heart began to beat rapidly at the sight of him. Music was pouring out of the house. She could hear the heavy beats of the bass even out here on the driveway. The lights from the house seemed to illuminate Charlie from behind. He glowed softly.

"Stacey, let me explain."

"You don't have to explain. It isn't any of my business."

"I'm trying to move on."

Stacey was brought up short. The words swirled in her head. She hadn't been expecting for Charlie to say that.

Taking advantage of her silence, he said, "We're over. I mean, you made it clear. Then Tony tells me you two are dating. I can't really sit around and pine for you any longer, can I?"

"No. I guess not."

"So, Adele was interested and I had never given her a chance before because of my father. So I thought I would."

"Isn't that falling directly into what your father wants?" Stacey asked.

Charlie shrugged. "Maybe. I guess so. I don't care, Stacey. I'm tired. Fighting against my dad like this is downright exhausting. I don't want to do it any longer."

Stacey couldn't keep the bitter tone out of her voice. "So, you'll just date her because she's around and your father already approves."

"No, no, you don't get to do this." He shook his head. "*You* left. You left *me*, remember? Now that I'm moving on, you don't get to be angry about it."

"I'm not angry."

"Yes, you are. Did you expect me to just be miserable for the rest of my life?"

"I expected you to reach out to me after I broke up with you!" Stacey snapped. "You seemed completely fine with the fact I had dumped you. And out of all the people to move on with, you pick Adele. The same woman you made clear that you had no interest in!"

"It doesn't concern you, Stacey! What I do now isn't any of your business! As for why I didn't contact you, I thought that was what you wanted! You broke up with me! I wasn't going to crawl around after you because you didn't want me any longer."

The two of them stared at each other. Charlie's eyes were wide. He had shifted in the middle of his rant. Half of his face was covered in shadows now. Behind him, Stacey could see Adele breaking through the edge of the crowd.

"Maybe you were right," Charlie whispered.

"About what?"

"Maybe we are just from two different worlds."

Stacey felt the air get sucked from her lungs at Charlie's words. She didn't have a chance to reply.

Adele had slinked up to Charlie. She wrapped her arms around his waist and rested her chin on his shoulder.

"Everything okay?"

"Yes. I'm just going, actually. Have a good night," Stacey replied stiffly.

She turned around and headed toward the gate, leaving Charlie behind.

Stacey shoved the money for the cab fare into the driver's hand and stepped out into the humid night. Above her, the apartment complex seemed to sag under the weight of its occupants. Without Tina living with her, the place seemed to have lost that little magic touch that had made Stacey feel so kindly toward it. She had once felt so victorious when Charlie had saved it from being knocked down and rebuilt. Now looking at it, Stacey wouldn't have cared if the entire thing was smashed to the ground.

Up in her apartment, Stacey went directly to her bed and fell into it with what felt like all the exhaustion in the world. Her window had a view of another building. From here, she could see someone's light on in the bathroom.

She was to go back to work on Monday. Tony had already given her more days off than she probably should have gotten. At the time, Stacey hadn't thought much of it. She had been too involved with Tina and making sure she was okay. Now that she was thinking about it, however, she wondered if she had been taking too much from Tony. The time off, the payment of the hospital bills and Tina's nursing home – she had been thrilled that Tony had been helping her so much.

But Stacey could practically hear Allison in her head. *You sit there and lecture me for wanting to snag a billionaire yet have no qualms about taking money from Tony.* The worst part was that Stacey had no argument back.

Everything she was starting to get on track had seemingly veered right off the rails. Stacey had somehow let Tony sweep in and start taking care of things. She wanted to date him. But she had to make sure he understood that she wasn't dating him for the handouts.

Tomorrow, she thought sleepily, *I'll figure it out tomorrow.*

Chapter Two

"You really didn't have to get me this," Stacey protested as Tony draped the necklace around her neck.

"Don't be silly. Of course I did. When I saw it, I thought that it would bring out your features beautifully," Tony said in a low voice, dragging his fingers gently across her neck.

The touch made her shiver. She closed her eyes for a moment before protesting feebly. But Tony didn't seem to be listening to her anymore. He was moving over to the poolside bar.

It was the middle of the week. Stacey had returned to work on Monday. If her co-workers cared that Tony had given her the time off, they didn't show it. For some reason, this bothered her more than it should have. Why were none of them, including Ms. Stark, bothered that Tony had given someone new so much time off?

"Want another?"

"No, I'm okay." Stacey held up her own unfinished drink.

This was her first time at Tony's place in the city. It was a penthouse suite, like Charlie's, only it was on the other side of town. He had a pool to himself here, and they were currently lounging next to it. The sun had gone down. The sky had streaks of orange shooting through it.

When Tony had invited her over, Stacey had promised herself to talk to him about how she didn't want him to spend any more money on her. Yet she hadn't gotten a chance to bring it up. Tony had taken her on a tour around his place and then given her the necklace. It felt rude to turn it down.

She fingered the necklace again. It was beautiful, lined with sapphires. In the back of her mind, Stacey wondered what it would fetch if she were to sell it. She quickly pushed the thought out of her head.

"I'm going out of town this weekend," Tony said as he sat down next to her. "I know I mentioned that before. I pushed it off to make sure you were okay, but I really must go this time."

"Back to China?"

"Somewhat," he smiled. "I own a very small island off the coast of mainland China. I have family that lives there. I'll be tending to business in Shanghai and spending time with them."

Stacey couldn't imagine owning an entire island. "Wow," she breathed, "that sounds lovely."

"It is. My family can come and go as they please, but they enjoy the peace and quiet. It will be good to see them again." He leaned back in his chair and looked out at the pool.

Somewhere in the distance there was a boom of thunder. Stacey studied Tony's face. In the darkness, she could just make out the curve of his jaw and his lips. As if sensing that she was staring at him, Tony turned to look at her.

His eyes flicked up to hers. Their gazes locked. Then Tony leaned across the small space between the two of them and kissed her. Like every touch from Tony, a warmth shot through her body. Tony cupped the side of her face with his hand and his tongue slid into her mouth.

Their kiss grew deeper. Anything that Stacey had been thinking about was quickly washed away with Tony's touch. His cologne filled her brain and she pressed her hands against his chest. His t-shirt curled around her fingers as she pressed her mouth against his.

Hungrily, Tony rubbed his hands down her sides. Stacey could feel her heart hammering against her chest. He pulled away from her suddenly. The two of them were out of breath. Something about Tony, being around him, touching him like this, always made Stacey feel as if her head was in a fog.

He took her hand and moved toward one of the lounge beds he had by the pool. It was white and had a sheet of fabric that shielded it from view. Stacey had commented about it when she had first come out on the patio. Tony had explained it was nice to tan or nap on.

Now she could see it was going to be used for a different purpose.

When they got close to it, Tony pushed her down onto the lounge bed. Stacey fell down on it as he climbed on top of her. He pressed his mouth against hers. His tongue probed hers as they both yanked each other's clothes off.

Stacey could feel how wet she was. Tony's stiff cock pressed against her thigh. The humid night air weighed down on the two of them. There was another clap of thunder in the distance. Tony ran a finger down her pussy which made her gasp in pleasure. He grunted as he slid his dick into her.

Then he was fucking her. One hand was tangled in her hair, pulling on it. His other hand was propping himself up as he thrust inside of her. Stacey wrapped her legs around his waist. She wanted him to go deeper and harder. She wanted him to make her finish around his cock.

She liked the sound of their flesh slamming against each other. Stacey liked how Tony would close his eyes when he moaned. She liked feeling his hands pulling her hair. His mouth came down around her tits, sucking and biting on her nipples as he vigorously fucked her. She could feel her own orgasm mounting.

Tony let out a loud moan. He grunted – once, twice, a final third time – as he thrust his cock deep inside of her and came. Stacey could feel his climax roll through him. He was shivering with his eyes closed. His mouth was clamped around one of her nipples as he came.

Stacey held him as he climaxed. After a minute, Tony rolled off of her. He lay there next to her out of breath. Part of Stacey couldn't help but feel a little disappointed. She told herself to stop. So what if she hadn't gotten to finish? She had still enjoyed herself, right? That was all that mattered.

Tony turned to look at her. Stacey offered up a wan smile. Tony's eyes were shining.

"I had an idea."

"What?"

He propped himself up. The humidity of the night was cooling off due to the storm rolling in.

"When I come back from China, I'll bring my family here."

"What?" Stacey asked, surprised.

"You can meet them. I won't ask you to come to the island. I know you don't want to leave Tina. So I'll bring them here for you to meet."

Stacey's eyes widened. "Meet your family? Don't you think that it's a little… fast?"

"Is it?" Tony wondered aloud and reached for her hand. "But I want you to meet them. I think you would really like them. Besides, I wanted them to come visit me for a while."

"Who would be coming?"

"My mother. My father died when I was younger. Some cousins. My older sister."

Stacey's head swam. "I didn't know any of this."

Tony brushed his lips gently across her own. The touch was as light as a feather.

"You'll really like them," he whispered. "We should get inside now before it rains."

Stacey nodded as Tony slid off the lounge bed and grabbed his clothes. She watched him stroll away from her. Her lips tingled from where he had touched her. Her fingers played with the necklace around her neck.

Tony was obviously into her. He was taking them being together seriously. She got up and dressed quickly on the patio before stepping into the kitchen. Tony was rummaging around in the fridge. The focused expression on his face looked cute on him. When he saw her, he flashed her a smile that made her knees feel weak. How could she say no to someone like Tony? He was kind and thoughtful. Hadn't he admitted to her earlier that he wasn't ready to settle down? Yet here he was, wanting Stacey to meet his family.

"Hungry?" he asked her.

"Yeah, I am. Thanks."

She went over to Tony as he pulled some food out of the fridge. He leaned over and kissed her. As their lips met, Stacey thought that maybe everything would work itself out in the end.

"Does it smell like old people?" Allison asked.

"What?"

Her sister wrinkled her nose. "Does it smell like old people?"

Stacey looked over at the nursing home. It was the first time Allison was going to be seeing it. For some reason, she felt nervous. Her sister had been on edge all day but wouldn't explain why. Stacey had to guess that it had to do with Jacob.

Not only that, but Stacey hadn't technically told Allison that Tony was paying for everything for Tina. She knew that Allison would be furious. It would be the same song and dance about the fact that Stacey was just like her, using money from a rich person to get what she wanted.

They got out of the car. Allison walked toward it as if she was walking to her own funeral. Stacey sighed.

"What?" Allison asked.

"It's just a nursing home. Don't be so dramatic."

"Are you kidding me right now?" Allison hissed. "Don't you remember my first-grade field trip?"

"Oh my God," Stacey groaned, "you're still not over that?"

In first grade, Allison had been taken to a nursing home to sing Christmas carols for the residents there. According to her, the sight of the old people not knowing where they were, all reaching out for her or calling her name in confusion, had been enough to scar her for life. Stacey tried not to roll her eyes.

They entered the nursing home. Allison fell silent when they stepped into the lobby. She took one look around and then pulled Stacey back before she could reach the desk.

"You can't afford this place."

"What?"

"You heard me," Allison said, "You can't afford it. You have that boyfriend of yours paying for it, don't you?"

Stacey didn't answer. She hadn't thought that Allison was going to guess right upon entering. Her sister took the silence as an answer. She was right.

"My God, sis. Never thought you had it in you. Using a man for his money." She raised her eyebrows.

Stacey could feel herself start to blush. "It isn't like that."

"It isn't? So he's paying for this place and what – you guys are just friends?"

"No. I mean…"

"So, you're fucking him." The delight in her voice was unmistakable.

"Keep your voice down!" Stacey snapped.

But Allison was grinning. "That is just rich. Well, I have to admit I am flattered that you decided to try things out my way."

"I am not trying things out your way."

"Really? What's the difference between you and me now?"

Stacey got very close to her sister. She could smell her sister's perfume. It was new. Probably designer. A gift from Jacob, no doubt. Her mind flashed to the necklace she had shoved in her drawer back at home.

"Yes, Tony paid for this place. But I am doing what I can to make sure our grandmother is in the best place possible and *this* is the best place for her. I am not going to put her in some shithole. You get it?"

"I get it. I do." Her sister pitched her voice down low. "Just make sure you don't lose yourself in the process."

Stacey didn't get a chance to reply. Her sister had turned around and gone to the desk, asking to see Tina. Her throat felt very dry. It was unlike Allison to be accepting of something. The fact that she had accepted it and merely added a cryptic warning had shaken Stacey.

After a few minutes of waiting, they were led to Tina's room. Tina was rolled up to the window and was reading a book. Sunlight poured in through the window. From here, Stacey could see outside. The garden was filled with people doing activities. She could see a small group of women doing yoga off to the side. The chess tables were filled with people as well.

Rebecca, the nurse who had helped Tina settle in, was in the doorway. Stacey turned to her.

Quietly, she asked, "Why isn't she outside in the garden?"

"I tried. But she wanted to stay inside. She said it was too hot."

That was unlike her grandmother. The heat had never seemed to bother her before. Allison had gone over to Tina and was talking to her in a low voice. Stacey couldn't hear what she was saying.

"Is she settling in okay?"

"She forgets often how she got here. Her short-term memory is poor. We have been working with her to try to keep her mind engaged. Coloring. Puzzles. Things like that. Her long-term memory is intact though."

"That's good at the very least."

"Well, if you have any questions, let me know. Feel free to take her to the gardens if you can get her to agree to it. The fresh air might do her some good."

Stacey nodded and Rebecca left them. There was a small TV in the room which was on. Even though Tina had access to probably tons of channels, it was on the weather channel. This small detail made Stacey's chest hurt.

Allison sounded tired, as if she had repeated herself already a few times, "No, this is my first time here."

"No, it isn't," Tina replied. "Weren't you here earlier? You wanted to go to the garden. Or was that your sister?"

Before Allison could get angry, which she always seemed to do instead of getting sad, Stacey stepped in. "Yeah, that was me."

Allison glared at Stacey who ignored it. She sat down next to Tina. The three of them spoke. The conversation was hardly a conversation. Tina's memory was fading quicker with each passing visit, it seemed. She would forget things mid-sentence. Conversations would die on her lips. It was a struggle. Stacey was used to it. Allison, however, left at one point.

"Will you wait right here?" Stacey asked her grandmother who nodded mutely.

She found her sister down the hall. She was leaning against the wall and was staring into one of the rec rooms. Allison was drumming her nails against the wall. Stacey noticed she had fake nails on. They were a bright purple. Currently they were more of a purple blur as she drummed them against the wall.

"Hey, what are you doing?"

"I can't do this," Allison gasped.

"Do what?"

"This." She gestured around her. "We can't even talk to her. You've noticed that, right?"

"Of course I have."

"We can't even talk to her," Allison repeated. "How can her mind have gone so quickly just like that?"

Stacey hesitated and then leaned against the wall. "It wasn't that quick. Her mind has been going for a while now. The seizure just moved the progress along a bit faster. But it was going to happen anyway."

Allison made a strange noise. Stacey knew it well. It was the noise her sister made when she didn't want to cry. Without thinking, she pulled Allison in for a hug which her sister reciprocated without hesitation.

Stacey couldn't recall the last time they had hugged. They were always fighting about something. But for once in their lives, there was no bickering. There was only sadness about their grandmother.

Chapter Three

"Tony, we need to rethink this money situation. I just don't feel as if I can take any more gifts from you. I appreciate everything you have done for my grandmother and the kindness you have given me. But I just can't…" Stacey shook her head. "Sounds so cheesy."

She was driving over to Tony's place that Friday night. After Tony had announced that he was going to be bringing his family into town this weekend, he had been gone all week in Shanghai. He had landed an hour ago. Stacey was determined to speak to him before his family came into town.

Her sister's warning had echoed in her head. It was probably the first time that Allison had warned her about anything, and Stacey couldn't stop thinking about it. Her sister constantly lost herself in men, didn't she? Stacey had seen it first hand over the years. She would alter and change her personality to match whatever billionaire she was trying to win over. Clearly, she was worried the same would happen to Stacey.

"I'm just going to tell him not to buy me anything else," Stacey said aloud.

It sounded simple enough. Yet why was she so nervous? Tony had never been cruel to her. But she knew there was iron underneath that skin. There had to be, to do the sort of business he did. She had never been nervous about that with Charlie.

At the thought of Charlie, Stacey told herself not to go down that road. She had been doing well at not thinking about the fact he was with Adele. If she dwelled on it, she found herself growing angry. All she could hear was what he had mumbled to her before Adele had appeared. His admission that perhaps they were from different worlds after all seemed lodged into her skull.

"Tony isn't Charlie," she said to herself as she stopped at a red light.

And that was a good thing. Surely, that was a good thing.

Her car looked like a hunk of scrap metal in the parking lot of Tony's complex. If Charlie's place had been luxurious, Tony's apartment complex was downright otherworldly. It looked as if it belonged in a science fiction novel. Everything was decorated with different colors and strange sculptures that made no sense to Stacey. The wealth was displayed at every stop to Tony's place. Even the elevators looked as if they were made of pure gold.

The elevator didn't take her directly to Tony's living room. Instead it opened into a beautiful hallway.

Mirrors lined the walkway to the door. Secretly, Stacey hated it. Seeing herself in all those mirrors only reminded her of everything she hated about her body.

She reached the door and knocked. It was slightly ajar, which she found odd. She knocked again but Tony didn't answer.

"Tony? I'm going to come in, okay?" Stacey called before pushing the door open slowly.

No one answered. The hallway was empty. Stacey was going to turn around and call Tony to make sure she had the time right when she heard someone laugh. It was a distant laugh, and distinctly female.

Standing there, she suddenly flashed back to coming home and seeing Jake with another woman. Their limbs had been entwined and he had been thrusting into her with a passion that Stacey hadn't seen from Jake in a long time.

She was thinking about this now as she walked down the hallway. Stacey tried to prepare herself for the image of Tony on top of another woman. Of course he would have gotten bored of her. They were from different worlds too, weren't they? She must have been a glutton for punishment.

A woman came around the corner and almost collided into her. She was shorter than Stacey with long, black hair, draped around her shoulders. There was something severe about her face - she looked exactly like Tony.

"Who are you?" she demanded in clipped English.

Stacey was at a loss for words. Luckily, she didn't have to answer. Tony came around the corner as well. When he saw her, he grinned.

"Great! You're here. This is my sister, Michelle. Michelle, this is Stacey, the woman I'm seeing."

Stacey, who moments ago thought she was going to catch Tony cheating on her, suddenly felt foolish. She held out her hand for Michelle to shake. Tony's sister did so but there was a look of slight disgust on her face as if she were smelling fish right under her nose.

"Nice to meet you," Stacey said.

Michelle made a small noise in the back of her throat and looked Stacey up and down. The look was not kind. Stacey wanted to be anywhere else but here. Tony grabbed her hand and steered her away from Michelle toward one of the lounge rooms.

"I thought they were arriving this weekend," Stacey whispered.

"Slight change of plans. It made the most sense this way. My mom and a couple of cousins came as well."

"Great," Stacey replied although she didn't mean it.

Out the window went her plan to discuss money with Tony. She was swept into the room where his mother sat. She was sitting by the window, sipping a cup of tea. She was extremely thin and looked as if she were only thirty years old. When she saw Stacey, she smiled thinly.

Behind Tony's mother were two of his cousins. One was a man who looked more like Tony's brother than cousin. The other was another woman with a round face and large eyes. She was the only one to smile warmly at Stacey.

"This is my mother, Ai. My cousin, Chen." He pointed to the male cousin who nodded at her, "And my other cousin, Mei."

Ai said something in Mandarin that of course Stacey couldn't understand. Chen laughed. It wasn't a kind laugh. Stacey stood next to Tony stiffly. He replied swiftly and his mother fell silent.

"Can I use your bathroom?" Stacey asked him, desperate to get out of that room.

Tony nodded and she left quickly. She went down the hallway and hesitated. On a whim, she decided to go to the bathroom on the other side of the penthouse. It would offer more privacy than being right outside the room with the family that seemed to already not like her.

She closed the bathroom door behind her. This side of the house was silent. She closed her eyes and took a deep breath. Okay, so Stacey hadn't been expecting Tony's family until this weekend. That really didn't matter, right? She knew they were going to be here. They were just here a bit early. Why was she panicking?

She knew the answer deep down. She was panicking because this entire relationship felt as if it were going way too fast for her liking. Already meeting Tony's family felt crazy to her. What was his hurry? To go from saying he didn't want to settle down to someone who now was introducing her to his family didn't make any sense in the least.

Stacey turned and stared at herself in the mirror. Allison had been right; things were out of control. At this rate, she had already lost track of herself. She needed to find a way to stop this before it got ridiculous.

She was about to leave when she heard low voices in the hallway. Stacey pressed her ear against the door. She could hear Tony talking. His voice was rising and falling as if he were irritated. Someone else replied. Stacey strained her ears.

"What is wrong with you?"

"Michelle, stop," Tony replied firmly in English. "I have no idea why you are all overreacting like this."

"I am used to meeting your flavor of the month," Michelle snapped, "but not someone like her! Do you see how she looks? She is double the size of me. Are you bored of the models you usually chase after? Or are you trying to piss off our mother because she's bothering you to settle down?"

A sick feeling was wriggling its way from Stacey's stomach. She knew she should let them know she was here in this bathroom but she felt frozen in place.

"I am not trying to piss off our mother," Tony finally spoke, "and her size shouldn't affect what you think of her. I wasn't expecting much from Mother or our cousins. But I thought you were better than that, Michelle. I really did."

There were footsteps of Tony marching off. She heard Michelle mumble something she couldn't make out before taking off as well. Stacey exhaled slowly.

Talk about a terrible situation.

She left the bathroom and walked back to the room where Tony's family was. The conversation ceased when she stepped inside. Tony went to her side and grabbed her hand, smiling at her as if nothing was wrong. As if his entire family didn't think she was some sort of temporary stop in Tony's dating career.

Even though he was smiling at her, Stacey couldn't help but remember that his sister had said she had met his girlfriends before. What she thought had been special wasn't that special after all. *Then none of this matters,* she told herself firmly, *I'm freaking out over nothing.* She couldn't make them like her after all. If they were convinced Tony wasn't serious about her, Stacey couldn't change that.

The conversation was stilted. There was a language barrier with Tony's mother. Tony did most of the translating. Mei spoke in broken English and Chen hardly spoke at all. It was Michelle and Tony who did the most speaking.

An hour passed before Stacey felt as if she could excuse herself with needing to get home for the night. Tony nodded and was about to show her to the door when Michelle offered to do it. He looked surprised but allowed Michelle to escort Stacey out.

Once they were alone, Michelle turned to look at Stacey. Her eyes were as dark as Tony's. She was staring at Stacey steadily.

"My brother seems quite taken with you," she finally said.

Stacey nodded, unsure of what to say.

Michelle looked away from her and flicked her hair back over her shoulders. "My brother took what my father had and grew it. He tripled the size of the small company our father had. When he died, Tony promised him it would be a glorious company. A company that stays in the family."

"If you think Tony has any plans to give me any hand in the company, I'm afraid you're mistaken," Stacey replied.

"No, I don't think he is going to do that. I think you will ask for it."

Stacey let out a dry laugh, "I have absolutely no interest in Tony's company."

Michelle narrowed her eyes. "Don't you? Tony told me what he did for you. For your sick grandmother. He has an iron will when it comes to business but a frail heart when it comes to people he cares about."

Stacey crossed her arms. She could feel her irritation quickly bubbling underneath her. When she had left Charlie, she had thought she was done with the strange workings of the rich and their dynamics. But now here she was, dealing with the same shit only a different family. *Out of the frying pan and into the fire,* Stacey thought glumly.

Michelle went on, "He won't marry you. You understand that, surely? Tony wants my mother to approve of whomever he decides to marry. She won't ever agree to you."

"What is it with you rich folks constantly getting into each other's business? Is it because you have everything at your fingertips so you have to make up some drama?"

Michelle's eyes widened slightly at Stacey's words. Then her mouth pressed into a thin line.

Irritated, Stacey went on, "For your information, I really do like Tony. He's kind. He's thoughtful beyond belief. But these sort of inner family politics – they don't interest me. I don't understand it. Where I come from with my family, we care about each other. We don't try to backstab or plot and plan. I guess that is where the money makes a real difference."

Before Michelle could reply, Stacey opened the door and left.

Chapter Four

The silence of the apartment seemed to weigh on Stacey like a thick blanket. She locked the door behind her and stood in the living room. The chair where Tina used to sit was sunken in from years of use. The couch where Allison used to sleep looked untouched. Something about it depressed her. Stacey realized for the first time in her life that she missed her sister.

She sat down on the couch and turned on the TV. The weather station popped up. A man was pointing out another summer storm about to rip through later that night. Stacey sighed and closed her eyes.

She must have fallen asleep because soon enough she was dreaming. She was back on the night of her parents' death, young and naïve. She was bent over her homework, trying to solve a math problem. But the numbers on the page kept swirling around and changing. It made it almost impossible to focus.

Next to her, Allison was unchanged. She wasn't a child, like Stacey. She was stretched out in between two chairs and was texting someone on her new phone. Her fingers swept over the touch screen rapidly.

"You should be doing your homework," young Stacey said to older Allison.

Her sister scoffed, "Lame."

"It's not."

Allison looked up at her. Her eyes were glowing a bright purple. Stacey shifted uncomfortably in the dining room chair.

"You run and you run," her sister said. "Why? What are you running from?"

Stacey didn't get to reply. Charlie stepped into the room. He was staring at her and said nothing. Behind him was Tony.

"You aren't supposed to be here," Stacey said to the two of them.

There was a loud noise from the living room. She got out of her chair and ran to the living room. Time seemed to slow down. Behind her, Allison kept texting on her phone. Charlie and Tony gave chase. As Stacey came into the living room, she saw her parents' bodies on the floor. She tried to scream, but no noise came out.

She spun around to get Tina – to try to tell her what was going on. But at her feet lay her grandmother. Her chest wasn't rising or falling. Stacey fell to her knees and tried shaking Tina awake. She didn't budge.

"What are you running away from?" Allison repeated from the dining room as Tony and Charlie stared at her. "What are you going to do about it?"

Stacey woke up with a gasp. Her eyes fluttered open to see the weather channel flickering on the screen. She could hear the rain pounding steadily on the roof. The clock showed an hour had passed. Her mouth felt as if it was filled with cotton. She had a headache.

The dream, once so vivid, was already drifting away from her. Stacey tried to hold onto it, but it was gone like water through her fingertips. She couldn't recall what had jolted her awake like that.

She went to get some water and something for her headache. Stacey then looked out the window and watched the rain drench the city. Tony hadn't called her since she had left. Had Michelle told him what she had said?

Yet Stacey had meant what she had said. What was it about Charlie's and Tony's families that made them poke and prod their way into their families' lives? Charlie, who had to deal with a father who wanted him to marry Adele. And Tony, who wouldn't marry anyone without Ai's approval. Stacey would always like more money, but would she want it at the risk of having her family rule her life?

Not like that mattered. There was no one left in her family besides her grandmother and her sister. There were a few distant cousins scattered around the country but no one she considered close.

A sudden knock on the door snapped Stacey out of wondering what to do. She wondered who it could be. She hoped it wasn't Tony following her home to try to talk about his family. She thought her head would pop if she had to deal with that right now.

Stacey opened the door and blinked in surprise. Allison stood in front of her. Her hair was wet from the rain and stuck to her face. Her dress was soaked through and her make-up was running.

"Are you okay?" Stacey asked.

Allison beamed and stuck out her hand toward her. She wiggled her fingers. Stacey looked down to see a gigantic ring on her sister's hand. The diamond glowed in the dim light of the hallway. She knew what Allison was going to say before she did.

"Jacob asked me to marry him!" she announced and then pushed her way past Stacey into the apartment.

"What?" Stacey replied numbly.

Allison spun in her heels. It was a childish gesture, one that Stacey hadn't seen her do since they were young. Her arms were outstretched and she was smiling.

"He asked me to marry him!" she repeated in a singsong voice.

"And you said yes?"

"Of course I said yes!"

"But..." Stacey tried to find the right words to convey how she was feeling. "But he's so... you know..."

Allison stopped spinning and waved her hand as if she was batting Stacey's feeble protests aside. "He's worth so much money, Stacey."

"That seems really wrong. Like not to be a judge of moral character but…"

Allison came over to her and gripped her by the shoulders. "He's worth so much money," she repeated. "We don't have to rely on Tony or anyone else. I can pay for anything Tina needs. I can get you out of this dump. Everything is going to change. You can come with me. We can travel the world together."

"I don't want to travel the world, Allison. And it isn't as if we aren't still relying on other people. We're relying on Jacob now, aren't we? That's the same thing. I don't want to travel the world on his money."

"Fine. Stay here then." Her sister's tone was flippant. "But we don't need Tony to pay for our grandmother to stay in that nursing home."

"Right, but Jacob will be," Stacey pointed out. "Nothing has changed." She pressed her fingers against her eyelids. "God, what are we both doing? How did shit get so far off track?"

Allison's arms went limp and fell away from Stacey's shoulders, "What do you mean?"

"I mean, we aren't doing anything for ourselves, are we? You're marrying a guy for his money. I've been accepting gifts from Tony because I'm too afraid of hurting his feelings. That isn't how life works. This isn't what Tina wants for us."

"What? Now you're an expert on what she wants for us?"

"Don't get mad. I don't feel like fighting about this, Allison. Seriously. You can't marry Jacob. You don't even *like* him."

"Well, what about you?" Allison retorted. "What are you going to do about it? You expect me to call things off with Jacob but you're still accepting things from Tony. I've seen how you look at him."

"What does that mean?"

Her sister shrugged. "You don't care about him as much as you think you do."

"That isn't true."

"Yes, it is," Allison retorted. "Think about it and you'll know it to be true."

Stacey ran her fingers through her hair. "It's just his family. The rich don't have to worry about paying the bills or keeping a regular job. So they get caught up in family drama instead. Get used to it, sis. I left Charlie because of it. But Tony's family is just as strange and conniving."

"Then go back to Charlie."

"I can't," Stacey said with a pang in her chest.

And it was true. She couldn't leave Tony and go back to Charlie. How could she go back to him now? As Allison stared at her, Stacey felt clammy all over. She moved away from her and sat down on the couch.

"Well, I'm marrying Jacob. I'm sorry if you disagree but I've decided this already."

"Fine," Stacey said, exhausted. "I can't tell you what to do anymore. Not with my own life like this."

Allison opened and closed her mouth before finally replying. "Well. Fine. Alright then." Her tone was off, as if she wasn't sure what to do without a fight from Stacey.

"I have to leave him, don't I?" Stacey mumbled to herself and she knew it was true.

As much as she liked Tony, she was staying with someone who had family drama just like Charlie. The truth was that she didn't like Tony as much as she had liked Charlie. There was a thread connecting her with Charlie. Even if he didn't want her, Stacey couldn't pretend to like Tony more than she did just to try to get over Charlie.

"I like Tony," Stacey said aloud, "I do. But I don't think I like him as much as I fooled myself into thinking I did."

"Then you need to break up with him," Allison said simply.

"Yeah, I do." She had known it, deep down, the first time they had slept together and had been left wanting. She had just pushed it down.

"Well. I just came by to give you the news," Allison said.

"You're leaving already?"

"You have a guy to dump, don't you?"

Stacey sighed. "I hate how you word things."

"I know you do. But sometimes it gets through your head quicker than if I was nice about it." She stopped for a moment and looked back at Stacey. "That Charlie guy. Even if he was a dick when he was trying to ruin the apartment complex… I wouldn't write him off so soon."

Her sister left. Stacey watched her go. She wasn't sure how she was feeling. She couldn't believe Allison was going to be marrying Jacob. She winced at the thought of having to suffer through his boring tales. She also didn't trust him as far as she could throw him.

Yet, if anything, it was enough to spur Stacey into action. She couldn't keep deluding herself into thinking that if she kept at it she could be with Tony. It wasn't fair to him or herself.

Trying to prepare herself, she grabbed her phone.

"I was thinking we could all go out to dinner tonight," Tony was saying. "There is a French place I want to take my family to."

Stacey made a small noise from the back of her throat and looked down at her tea. Tony had come over to her place after she had finished up work that day. He was sitting across from her and had been talking non-stop since he had arrived. Normally, Stacey wouldn't have minded too much. But today, of all days, she was waiting for him to stop so she could end things.

For some reason, she was more nervous about breaking up with Tony then she had been with Charlie. Perhaps it was because she knew Charlie was a sweetheart through and through, whereas Tony always gave off the vibe that there was ice underneath everything.

"Tony," Stacey finally said.

Something in her tone must have alerted him to something because he finally fell silent.

Nervously, she went on, "It was nice meeting your family on Friday."

"Are you upset with me because I couldn't see you this past weekend?" Tony asked her.

"No. No, I'm not. I know you had a lot going on. So have I, with my sister. It's fine." She cleared her throat and tried to restart. "Meeting your family just made me realize that we are going quite fast."

"Are we?" Tony asked, looking surprised.

"Yes. Meeting family is usually a big step forward in a relationship. With that realization, I just think it would be better if we slowed down."

"Slowed down?"

Stacey's throat was going dry. She cleared it and tried to speak. "As friends. I think we would be better if we were friends."

Tony's eyes widened. Silence filled the space between them. For a few moments, he didn't say anything. Stacey looked back down at her tea.

"This is because of Charlie, isn't it?"

Startled, she looked up. "What?"

"You still care about him. I can tell, you know. Especially at that party. I can tell by the way you two look at each other. I thought you'd get over him once we got serious. But I can tell that isn't going to be the case."

Feeling as if a spotlight was shining directly on her, Stacey stammered out, "It isn't just Charlie."

He waved his hand as if he was dismissing anything else she had to say. "Charlie isn't good for you. You understand that, don't you? That's why you left him. I get you, Stacey. I understand where you're coming from. Your struggles are deep within. Starting from the bottom and working your way to the top."

"How?" Stacey asked. "No offense, Tony, but you and I come from different worlds just like me and Charlie."

"I took what my dad left me, and I turned it into something. What did Charlie do? His father had already built the company. He just took it over. Barely, I might add. His father wants nothing more than to get his hands back into the company. He's just too ill. If Charlie can't ward off his sick father, how can you expect him to really love someone like you?"

"Someone like me? What does that mean, exactly?"

"Someone poor," Tony said bluntly. "Someone from the bottom. Someone trying to get out of the bottom they were born into. I get that. I understand what you are trying to do. He doesn't. He never will."

"This isn't just about Charlie. Even without him in the picture, we wouldn't mesh well together. I can't take any more of your money either, Tony. I'll figure out someplace to put Tina, but –"

Tony shook his head. "No. Let your grandmother stay there. Because you'll come back to me, eventually. It might take some time, but you'll realize that Charlie isn't the type of man you want."

He stood up. Stacey felt speechless. What could she say to someone who clearly felt so cocky about the situation? To be so sure that she would run back to him filled her with an irritation she hadn't experienced before.

"See you around, Stacey," Tony said to her as he left the room.

A few seconds later, she heard the front door open and close. Stacey sat there in shock.

"That went great," she mumbled.

She thought about what Tony had said. Even though she thought it was a load of shit, his tone had been so casual and confident. He had hardly stopped to hear her out about why she didn't think they would work out. She really didn't like his assumption that she would change her mind and go back to him. Charlie was never that arrogant.

"It doesn't matter. We're over now at least," she said aloud to herself again.

What now? She had broken up with Tony, but it wasn't as if Charlie was lining up to date her again. She could almost picture him right now, tangled up with Adele, leaving kisses down her neck. The thought of it made her sick.

She regretted leaving him. She wished she had taken that risk and stayed with him to see things through. Now Charlie had moved on and although Stacey was happy she had left Tony, she was alone.

Her tea had gone cold by the time she snapped out of her thoughts. Her mind was whirling with thoughts of Tony and Charlie. She couldn't help but feel as if she had let a chance with someone she truly cared about slip through her fingers. Yet she couldn't deny that she had felt a pull toward Tony as well.

She also still had her sister on her mind. She wished that she could talk Allison out of marrying Jacob. It felt like a huge mistake. Yes, she would have money, but there was more to life than that. Jacob was a bore and seemed selfish. Not to mention there was a nagging feeling that Stacey couldn't shake as to why he was so keen to marry Allison.

She stood up from the table. It was late and her head was pounding. Better to go to bed early and try to get some sleep than struggle with her brain for hours.

Chapter Five

Stacey had been dreaming again when her phone woke her up. She had been running through a maze of trees, trying to catch up to someone when her eyes opened to her bedroom ceiling. On her night table, her phone vibrated loudly. In the quiet of the apartment, it felt as if someone was smashing a gong right next to her.

Her clock showed it was a little after two in the morning. Wondering what in the world her sister had gotten herself involved into this time, Stacey groggily grabbed her phone and answered.

"Hello?"

The voice at the other end spoke and everything changed.

Allison's fingers were wrapped around Stacey's own so hard that she dimly wondered if her bones were going to snap. It was a gesture that her sister used to do when they had stayed up late to watch horror movies together. It meant she was scared and was trying not to show it.

In front of them, they could do nothing but watch Tina's casket being lowered into the ground. Stacey felt as if all emotions had been drained out of her. She felt hollow staring at it. It hardly made sense that Tina was with them one night and gone the next. A heart attack had come out of the blue and snatched their grandmother away from them.

Next to her, Allison let out a noise that sounded as if she were being choked. Jacob was standing next to her dressed in all black. He had one arm wrapped around her shoulders. For once in his life, he was silent.

Allison began to cry. She turned to Stacey – not Jacob – for comfort. Jacob's eyes flickered over to her, but she just blinked back at him. What did he want her to do? Say no to her grieving sister? She stroked Allison's hair and looked around the small group of mourners.

She felt as if she was staring into a fishbowl. Perhaps it was because she felt so outside of herself right now that even the sight of both Tony and Charlie in the crowd didn't stir anything in her. Stacey wasn't sure if she was going to feel anything ever again.

A few people broke off and began to walk to their cars after saying good-bye to the two of them. Tina had outlived most of the people she had called friends. The small group that had arrived were people that Stacey and Allison had known.

Amanda came over to her. "Hey. It was a beautiful service."

"Thank you," Stacey replied, noting that Amanda had shown up with Brad.

"Can I do anything at all to help out? I can come over and cook," Brad offered.

"No, thank you. I really do appreciate it. But I'm alright."

Brad and Amanda said good-bye. Stacey watched them go. Allison moved away from her and furiously wiped her face.

"Fuck. I'm sorry. I told myself I wasn't going to cry."

"It is quite alright, dear." It was Jacob who spoke up, pulling Allison toward him.

She nodded and looked back at Stacey. "Are you okay? You seem…"

"I'm fine."

Her sister narrowed her eyes, clearly not believing her. Stacey didn't know what to say. She wanted to tell Allison that she hadn't felt anything in her heart or soul since the call that Tina had died. Nothing seemed to affect her. It was as if she had been drained completely of emotion. She hadn't even cried. A switch had been flipped, leaving her empty. Nothing mattered.

But her old boss, William, came up to her just then. Besides, Stacey wouldn't have said such things around Jacob.

After giving his condolences, William asked, "No wake then?"

"No. Tina always said she didn't want one," Stacey replied. "She said she didn't want a bunch of people crying over her over poorly made finger food."

"Although I did offer to take everyone out for dinner," Jacob chimed up.

Stacey lazily turned her head to look at him. His mouth, which had been opened to most likely drone on again, shut promptly when he saw the look on Stacey's face. Allison, sensing turmoil, pulled on his sleeve. The two of them turned away from her and headed off toward the parking lot.

"Well, if it's what she would have wanted," William said, oblivious to the moment.

"It is, thank you."

"Listen, Stacey," he cleared his throat, "I know you have a new job. And I bet it's great. But with the money I got from selling the restaurant, I've been debating a new business venture."

"Have you?"

"Yes. I won't bore you with the details now. But how about I call you sometime and we can discuss it? Perhaps you'd be interested and you'd want to give it a shot. Build something from the ground up."

Stacey, hardly hearing him, agreed. William beamed and said good-bye. A couple of Allison's friends came up after to chat. They left after a few moments. The sky was starting to darken with another storm. Stacey stared at the sky. She felt rooted to the spot as if she was going to grow into the soil right there next to Tina's grave.

"Stacey."

She turned her head to see Charlie. There was a time he would have pulled something out of her. An accelerated heartbeat. Her head spinning at the sight of how handsome he looked. Right now, however, she felt nothing as she looked at him.

He hesitated and then walked up to her. He looked tired. His eyes were ringed with dark shadows. He had more stubble on his face than Stacey had ever seen on him before. He ran his fingers through his hair which was slightly messy from the wind.

"I'm sorry for coming but I knew how much Tina meant to you," he said to her, keeping a safe distance between the two of them.

"I appreciate you coming," Stacey said for what felt like the millionth time that day.

Charlie took a step toward her. "Stacey, truly… I am so sorry this happened. I know that you had just gotten her settled into the home. For a heart attack to come out of the blue like that…"

"They normally do, don't they?" Stacey's voice was clipped and sounded distant, as if it belonged to someone else.

Charlie looked slightly taken aback. "I suppose so."

If she had been herself – truly herself – she would have thrown her arms around him and told him to come back to her. It sounded dramatic and perhaps it was. But Stacey wasn't herself. All she could do was stand there and look at Charlie as if he were worlds away.

He looked nervous now as he took another step toward her. They were close now. She could make out the finer details of his face. The way he was looking at her as if he were approaching a deer in the wild. The way his chest was rising and falling quickly.

"I have to talk to you, Stacey."

"Not now. I don't want to discuss it now." She cut him off brutally.

But he didn't let it drop. "Listen, last time. At the party. Things went south and I said some things I didn't mean."

"I don't care about that anymore. Did you come here to make this death all about you?"

Charlie looked aghast. "What? No."

"You told me what you thought about us. You agreed with me that we were too different. So why are you here now, trying to tell me you didn't mean it?" Stacey's words came fast and hard, rolling off her tongue without thinking.

In the back of her mind, the part of her that usually spoke logic and reasoning was eerily silent. All Stacey wanted to do was push Charlie away from her. There was something that overwhelmed her being this close to him. The sight of him and the scent of him made her feel as if she was going to topple over a ledge.

"I know what I said," Charlie fought back, "but I was wrong. I was hasty. I just – I know you feel it. The connection we have."

Her eyes flickered over to her grandmother's grave. Tina, who had been yanked from this world so quickly, had taken the last bit of Stacey's will to keep fighting and keep trying.

Didn't she feel a connection with Charlie? She had. More than she wanted to admit. A week ago, if Charlie had come to her and said these things, she would have jumped at the chance. Now she just wanted to be away from him, away from everyone who had a part in her life that made her feel things. She didn't want to get hurt again. Stacey just simply didn't want to let anyone in.

"I have to go. Thank you again for coming, Charlie."

Stacey brushed past him. In the movement, their hands briefly touched. Something flickered deep in her heart, like a candle trying to illuminate darkness. But Stacey ignored it and walked away from him. The dark clouds had rolled in now, seemingly directly over the cemetery.

She saw Allison ahead of her, talking to a tall, dark-skinned man that seemed like a blast from the past. It was Jake. His head was lowered and he was talking to her. Allison's shoulders were hunched over and she was crying. Stacey didn't see Jacob.

Stacey didn't want to talk to her ex. She changed direction and wandered down one of the rows of gravestones. Better to let Allison handle Jake than herself. She stopped in front of a grave that was covered in weeds. It was obvious no one had been by in quite some time to pay this one a visit.

This is going to be all of us one day, Stacey thought glumly. Her parents were already in the ground. So was her grandfather. And now, so was Tina. For a spilt second, she could feel raw pain shoot through her body as if she had poured salt into a wound.

"Hey."

The wound sealed up at the sound of Tony's voice. Stacey looked up from the grave and turned around. Unlike Charlie, Tony looked the same. There were no dark circles around his eyes. No stubble. His hair was perfectly slicked back. Like Charlie, Stacey felt nothing at seeing him.

"You ran off before I could talk to you," he said.

Stacey didn't reply.

Tony came over to her and stood next to her. Together they stared at the grave where Stacey had stopped.

Finally, he spoke. "My grandfather had always been my biggest supporter. Everyone in my family, they didn't understand what I was trying to do. They thought it was crazy to keep working on the business and build it up. But he always believed in me. When he died, for a while, I felt nothing."

Stacey still didn't answer. She didn't know what he wanted her to say.

Tony went on, "It felt like everything had been yanked out of me. Everything that made me feel like a human was gone. I was struggling."

"Why are you telling me this?"

"I assume you're feeling the same way."

"Because we are so alike, right?" Her tone was frosty.

"Correct. Because we are more alike than you want to admit."

Stacey turned to look at him and crossed her arms. "I can't figure you out. You could have anyone in the world. Any sort of supermodel or high ranking business woman. Yet you seem to think that we are perfect for each other."

"And you don't? I don't want a supermodel. Or some rich woman my father picked out for me." The dig on Charlie was not lost on Stacey. "I want someone who knows what it's like to struggle and who wants more from life. So I made some mistakes with you. I can rectify that. I can change that. If you let me."

"I don't feel like dating anyone."

Tony's hands rested on her shoulders. "Because you're hurting and won't let yourself feel it. So let me take care of things. Come with me."

"Come with you where?"

"To paradise. To wherever you want. Stop fighting how you feel about me and come with me. Forget the shit here and come with me."

Stacey's eyes left Tony's and instead looked around the cemetery. In the distance, she could see Charlie. He was still standing where she had left him. He had wanted her, all of her. He had wanted to try it out again. She could go with him. Stacey could open her heart to Charlie and try it again.

Or she could run away with Tony. What was she really risking there? Even if Tony left her, it would sting but it wouldn't tear her apart as if she had taken a risk on Charlie. It was safer for her… and right now, after losing Tina, what she wanted was safe.

She tore her gaze away from Charlie and looked up at Tony.

"Fine. Let's go."

Chapter Six

"Hey! Get up!"

The voice broke through Stacey's sleepy fog. She rolled over and looked in the doorway of her room. At first she thought that she was imagining it.

"Seriously, you're still in bed? It's one in the afternoon."

"Allison?" Stacey asked, her throat as dry as parchment.

"The one and only. You were supposed to send a car to get me from the airport." Her tone was accusatory as she strolled into Stacey's bedroom.

"I forgot. I thought you were coming on Friday."

"It is Friday."

Stacey propped herself up in bed. How had she lost track of time like that? Although, admittedly, it was easy to do on the island. The last three months that she had been here had been a complete and total blur of long days doing nothing and long nights on the beach.

Allison was looking around the room. She hadn't seen her sister since the day of Tina's funeral. Her sister looked the same besides her hair. She had dyed it a bright blonde which contrasted with her dark skin.

She wrinkled her nose. "Jesus, Stacey, this room really needs to be swept up. Don't you have a maid or something?"

"I don't let her in here."

She did have a point though. As if she could see things through her sister's gaze, Stacey saw the mounds of clothes tossed on the floor. Things were strewn about the room. The vanity was crowded with different types of make-up and tons of perfume bottles. The closet was open with clothes spilling out onto the floor.

The windows had been thrown open in the room, allowing the breeze to roll through. From here, Stacey could see the ocean. It was a bright clear blue and still took her breath away. Her room allowed her to walk directly onto the beach. She usually moved between her bedroom and the beach throughout the day.

"Amazing beach house," Allison remarked. "I walked through it before I stopped by your room. You sleep in separate rooms from Tony?"

"I told you. We aren't dating."

"Right. So you just ran off with him the same night we buried our grandmother to this tropical paradise and have been what, playing chess with him at night?" Allison's tone was dry.

"Is Jacob with you?"

"No. He's at our own place getting ready for the wedding."

The wedding. Since coming here to the island that Tony owned in the Bahamas, she hadn't spoken often with Allison. When she did speak to her, Allison kept her updated on how things were going. Stacey had stopped speaking out about the wedding once she arrived on the island. It wasn't her business anymore. Nothing was.

"Nice of Tony to let us use his island for our big day though." Allison sat down on the edge of the bed. "He has enough guest houses for everyone and plenty of space to hold the wedding."

"Sounds great."

"I guess so." She was playing with the edge of one of Stacey's blankets with some expression on her face that Stacey couldn't make out. "What about you? You ran off so quickly. Sorta just fell off the map. And now here you are! Not dating Tony. Just... doing what, exactly?"

Something about Allison bursting in here and seeing her asleep in the afternoon surrounded by a messy room had Stacey on edge. Maybe it was the fact that she knew she wasn't at her best right now. Perhaps it was because it felt as if real life was finally creeping in on her, trying to yank her back into it. But Stacey would be dragged into it kicking and screaming.

"It's been great. Really lovely. Long days by the beach just relaxing. Best three months I've ever had."

"And you're okay with… with all of this? Tony paying for everything?"

"You're okay with marrying Jacob?" Her tone was openly hostile, challenging Allison.

To her surprise, Allison backed off right away. "Whatever you have to do, Stacey." She stood up.

"Leaving already?"

"Yeah, I should get back to the guest house. We are only two houses down from you. You'll stop by, yeah?"

She didn't wait for an answer and gave Stacey a little wave instead. She closed the door behind her. Stacey was left alone – and for the first time in three months felt as if she had just burst out of a thick fog.

She looked around the room, focusing on how completely messy it was. She hadn't bothered to clean up any of it. Would she have, even if she had remembered her sister was coming by? For some reason, Stacey had just assumed that Allison wasn't actually going to go through with the marriage.

But here they both were, on Tony's private island. It was true that it was perfect for a wedding. There were guest homes across the small island. There was a building in the center for events. Tony had bought the island a couple of years ago. He had told her that he liked taking his yacht out here. Sometimes he would bring groups of people here for vacations.

Yet no one else had been here since Stacey had come here. Tony came by when he could, working from his office on the other side of the island. Yet there were days at a time when he had to go back into the world of the living. Stacey remained behind, spending her days by the beach or reading books.

Once in a while, a reminder of life outside the island would try to get her attention. Allison would ask when she was coming back home. A mention of Charlie in passing by Tony, when talking about business, would make Stacey's heart feel as if it had stopped completely for a few seconds. At night, there would be times when she couldn't sleep because she knew Tina wouldn't have wanted her to grieve this way.

But it was easier to forget. It was easier to go swimming in the beautiful ocean than wonder how long she was going to stay here and what she was going to do afterward. This was her hideout. Stacey didn't want to leave it.

She swung her legs over the king-sized bed and padded into her bathroom. When she had first gotten here, she had marveled at how large and state of the art it was. Now, she barely looked at it as she brushed her teeth and stripped off her clothes.

In the shower, she let the hot water pound against her skin. Something that Allison had said kept bothering her. It was when she had mentioned Tony being in a different room than hers. It was true that they were in different rooms. Stacey hadn't given the two of them much thought, actually. She didn't consider them to be dating, but it was because she hadn't wanted to dwell on it.

She had slept with Tony a handful of times in the three months. Like every time, it was over quickly and left her feeling unsatisfied. There had been no improvement there. Stacey hadn't given it much thought. She had wanted that physical touch from someone some nights. Tony was nearby and it made the most sense.

For the first time since Tina died, a true and terrible emotion rose up inside of her as she stood underneath the shower head. It swept over her like a pure sickness, and for a second she thought she might throw up.

Then Stacey realized what she was feeling. It was a mixture of grief and shame. Grief over her grandmother. Shame at the fact that she had turned tail and run away from all her problems. She had run away from Charlie. Her sister. The entire life she had been trying to carve out back home.

Deep down, she had known what she was doing. But Stacey had buried it so far down and focused only on running away with Tony that it had been easy to trick herself.

She hadn't felt much since getting here. It was so easy to stick her head in the sand and waste her days with Tony. But seeing Allison had reminded her of a life outside of this tropical paradise. Her sister was going to marry someone for money. Wasn't Stacey hiding out here with someone whom she could never feel the way she did about Charlie?

Charlie – she had rejected him that day by Tina's grave. He wanted another shot, but she had been too terrified to let him in. She shut him down and ran away like a scared fool.

Stacey scrubbed her skin extra hard, lost in thought. She had to get out of here. She could leave with Allison. She'd find another job and go back home to her dingy little apartment.

She got out of the shower, dressed quickly, and left her bedroom. Allison had said she was nearby. She'd go see her. Try to talk to her about coming home with her.

But in the foyer, she ran into Tony. He was dressed casually. Spending so much time out here had turned his skin a deep tanned color.

"Saw your sister. Guess we should get ready for the rest of the guests arriving here later on."

"Yeah. I'm actually going to see her to say hi."

He frowned. "She said she came by to see you already. Said you were still in bed." He came over to her and wrapped his arms around her waist. "How are you?"

"Awake," Stacey mumbled, meaning it in more ways than just the one.

Tony laughed. "Well, that's good. Listen, with all the guests arriving, I was thinking I'd buy you something new to wear. Something nice. What do you think?"

She thought of the piles of clothes back in her room and mentally cringed. Tony had been buying her lots of things. She had accepted all of it, barely glancing at whatever he had tossed her way. She had let things get completely out of control.

"No, I'm okay," Stacey replied firmly. "I think I have enough clothes."

Tony frowned again. "Are you sure? We can find something."

"I'm good, really." She untangled herself from his grip and forced herself to smile. "I'm going to go see Allison again though. It's been three months after all."

Before he could say anything else, Stacey ducked past him and went out the front door. It was humid but beautiful. The palm trees looked as if they could touch the sky, which was a beautiful solid blue. There wasn't a cloud in sight. She could hear the ocean as she walked along the pathway to the other houses.

Imagine owning an island. Stacey hadn't given it much thought before. Honestly, ever since she'd arrived, she hadn't given much thought to anything besides trying to forget about Tina. She had been determined to seal off her emotions from anything that could cause her pain.

As she looked around, for the first time it really hit her that Tony owned this entire place. He was rich beyond belief. The yacht and the island alone would be something Stacey could never have afforded in three lifetimes. Yet Tony owned both and was content just letting her stay here. She had hardly walked around the island. She had been in the villa and the beach for most of her time here.

Now she turned the corner on the pathway and came to a row of the guest homes. These were a lot smaller than the main villa but still pretty to look at it. Allison was outside of one with her cellphone raised as if she was trying to get a signal.

"Hey," Stacey called out.

She looked over and waved. She lowered her phone and crossed the short distance toward Stacey.

"Look at you. Out and about."

"I get out and about here."

Allison laughed. "No, you don't. You've been hiding out here for months. You pretty much fled the country just so you didn't have to deal with things. I woke you up, didn't I?"

"Don't start. 'Waking up' is a bit of an exaggeration," Stacey said, unwilling to admit that Allison was right.

"Too late. I've started." She grinned and in spite of Stacey's mood, she found herself grinning back.

"So, come on. Show me around the guest villa."

"You haven't been in any of the guest houses?"

"No," Stacey admitted. "I haven't really left the main villa at all."

"Geez, you've really been doing nothing this whole time, haven't you?" Allison asked as they walked up the front steps.

"Not true," Stacey said defensively. "I know that Tony has this island here mainly for parties. 'The ultimate getaway place' is what he calls it."

"It's pretty impressive. Actually, Jacob is a bit jealous of it," Allison said over her shoulder as they stepped into the house.

Stacey didn't get to ask why he was jealous because Jacob was in the foyer. He was rummaging through a suitcase. He looked unchanged from the last time that Stacey had seen him at Tina's funeral.

"Allison, dear, have you…" He looked up and saw Stacey. "Oh. Stacey. Nice to see you again."

"Same to you," Stacey replied, not really meaning it.

Jacob straightened up. "I was looking for my laptop. I shoved it into one of the suitcases."

"The red one. I put it in our room."

"Ah, great. What would I do without you?" he said and leaned over to kiss the top of Allison's head before leaving without another word.

"He's usually a bit more…"

"Chatty?" Allison finished. "I know. I hope he's just nervous and isn't getting cold feet."

Stacey pulled her sister into the living room and lowered her voice, "Are you sure about this?"

"Oh no. No, no, no."

"What?"

"You don't get to do this now, Stacey. Not after you ran off and hid out with Tony on his *own private island*."

"I'm just worried. That's all."

"About what?"

"Well. Tony mentioned before at a party how this guy normally doesn't date… people like us."

Allison's eyes narrowed. "So, what, exactly? He's using me? For what, Stacey? I give him nothing. I have no money. I have no business ties to anything he could use me for. He gets nothing out of dating me besides me fawning over him. Perhaps that's what he wants. Someone just to fawn over him no matter what he says."

Stacey felt abashed and looked away. "Yeah, maybe."

"So, not another lecture. Okay? This is happening tomorrow night. That's that."

Stacey nodded, knowing there was nothing else that she could say to change Allison's mind. Not to mention that her sister did have a point. Stacey had been hiding out here, running away from real life. She couldn't exactly lecture Allison about marrying Jacob any longer.

"Great. Come on. Let me show you my dress. You are literally going to die," Allison said with a grin.

Chapter Seven

When Stacey arrived back at the villa later that night, she hadn't been expecting company. In hindsight, she should have. Allison and Jacob's wedding party could all fit on the island, which meant it had to be under two hundred people if each house was filled to the maximum. Tony was in the same social circle as Jacob, so guests were to be expected.

But when she stepped into the living room that night, she hadn't been expecting the guests to be Tony's family again. It was like accidentally walking onto a stage in the middle of a play. All eyes turned to her. Ai cleared her throat softly. Michelle's face looked the same. Chen wrinkled his noise a little. It was Mei who gave her a wave and a smile, which was more than Stacey had gotten last time.

Tony jumped to his feet quickly. He was holding a glass of whiskey. His hand was wrapped firmly around it, which was the only indication that whatever was going on here wasn't a good thing.

"Stacey. Nice time at your sister's?"

"Yes," Stacey replied. "She's very excited."

"Great." He came over to her and turned her to walk her out of the room. Stacey could feel the eyes of his family still on her.

"What is that about? Where did they come from?" Stacey whispered when they were in the hallway.

"Don't freak out."

"What does that mean?"

"Jacob invited them. It was supposed to be a surprise. A thank you for letting him use the island. He thought I hadn't seen them in over a year."

"Well, that was nice of him at least," Stacey said.

"Yeah, well. They aren't too happy that I have you here."

"Of course not," she mumbled.

Tony ignored her. "It isn't anything personal, Stacey. They just thought I'd have either married you or broken up with you by now."

"Isn't personal? Come on, Tony. I know what Michelle thinks of me at the very least. That I'm some fat woman you're taking pity on or something. She said she was used to meeting your girlfriends. So how many do you parade through to see if your family approves?"

"What? How do you –"

"I overheard the two of you back when I met them at your penthouse," Stacey admitted.

Tony's eyes widened slightly. "You should have told me. You shouldn't listen to Michelle. She just doesn't understand… what we have."

"What do we have?" Stacey heard herself say before she could stop herself. "What are we doing? They aren't going to approve of me, Tony. You know it. If you bring every woman you date by your family to find one that sticks, you're going to spend the rest of your life trying to please them."

"Stacey, wait." He grabbed her hand as she turned to leave. "What do you mean? 'What are we doing?' I thought we were doing just fine."

He was looking at Stacey with a pained expression on his face. Not for the first time in their three months together, Stacey wondered what went on in that mind of his. It was a rare glimpse to see what went on in his head. He was kind to her and always thoughtful. But Tony seemed to keep everything close to his heart, refusing to let her in, even when she had pressed him to open up.

"What do you want from us, Tony? Your mother won't approve of us marrying. So, what, you'll try to marry me anyway?"

"I was hoping that they would warm up to you. They don't even know you."

"They aren't going to warm up to me and you know it. I know it too."

"They just need to spend more time around you. Please."

Stacey wavered. She looked back in the direction of Tony's family with a growing sense of dread. Why couldn't she say no? It was as if the time she had spent here had wilted her.

"I have a headache," Stacey finally said. "I have to lie down. Tell your family I'm sorry."

She pushed past Tony, leaving him alone in the hallway.

Of course Stacey couldn't sleep. She tossed and turned in bed. Even the sound of the ocean, which was once so soothing, bothered her. She felt isolated here on this island, cut off from the rest of human kind.

That was her fault, though. This island that had once been her refuge from dealing with her own feelings and problems now felt like it had her chained to the ankles, dragging her down.

Unable to sleep, Stacey kicked off the sheets and got out of bed. She opened her door very slowly. She had no idea if Tony's family was still here. There weren't enough bedrooms for all of them to stay here, which meant they had to be in one of the guest homes at least.

Stacey flattened herself against the wall and crept down. The entire thing reminded her of when she was a child and used to creep downstairs to see if Santa had left presents under the tree.

She stopped at the end of the hallway. Tony's family members were all speaking in the foyer. As his family left, soon it was just Michelle and Tony.

Michelle was speaking rapidly in Mandarin. Stacey held her breath, hoping that the two siblings would switch to English. She should let them know that she was here. She knew that. But something kept her firmly rooted to the ground.

Finally, Tony spoke in English. "I'm exhausted, Michelle. Need to sleep."

"I just think you're wasting your time. She doesn't love you."

Stacey flinched. Tony answered in Mandarin.

Michelle went on in English, "Stop denying it. You keep trying to woo this woman for some reason none of us understand. But I can tell just by looking at her she loves someone else. The two of you have pulled the wool over your own eyes. She isn't going to marry you, Tony, even if Mother approved. So cut her loose. You're wasting your time. She's holding you back. You're supposed to be in charge of the business and instead you're rotting on this island with her."

With that, Michelle left the house. She heard the door slam shut. Stacey turned to go back to her room when Tony spoke.

"I know you're there."

She froze and then stuck her head out from the corner. Tony was leaning against the wall with his arms crossed. He looked exhausted for the first time since Stacey had met him.

"Sorry. For listening in."

"I'm not angry. Probably the only way you can get answers around here, right?"

Stacey didn't know what to say. She watched as Tony closed his eyes for a few seconds before opening them again to stare at her.

"Is it true?" Tony finally asked.

"Is what true?"

"What Michelle said. That you love someone else."

Stacey felt as if someone had pushed her in front of a speeding train. She could either let it smash into her and let it drag her away. Or she could leap out of the way and break free.

"Yes. I think so."

Tony sucked in a little bit of air through his mouth as if someone had punched him. Then he shook his head and said, "It's Charlie, isn't it? I don't get it. I don't understand why you're still wrapped up in him."

"I didn't know I was. I thought… I thought since he was seeing Adele that it was time to move on. It didn't make sense to be pining after him any longer."

"So, what, you came here?"

"That isn't the only reason I came here and you know it," Stacey replied. "I didn't want to be back home living in that apartment with my grandmother's ghost. All those memories. Allison is leaving too. She's getting married. It was all too much. So yes, I ran. I ran away with you. Maybe it was a hasty decision on my part, but I had to get my mind off all the things that were haunting me, and I don't just mean my grandmother. Sorry, bad joke…"

"You should have stayed," Tony said bitterly. "You should have stayed and gone off to fuck Charlie."

"Hey, that isn't completely fair. I told you before that I didn't think we were going to work out. And you knew even then that I was struggling with Charlie and how I felt about him. When I agreed to come with you, it wasn't because I… because I loved you or anything. I thought you knew that."

Tony pushed off the wall and walked over to her. He grabbed her shoulders. His thumbs dug into her skin. He held her there tightly, staring down at her.

"I told you when you broke up with me, if you remember," he said in a low voice, "that we belong together. We are two sides of the same coin."

"Let go of me," Stacey said, trying to keep her voice calm.

But Tony didn't. He kept speaking. "You're hung up on the illusion of Charlie. Not what he is really like."

"How would you know?"

"I just know. I just know!" He raised his voice suddenly.

Stacey yanked herself away from him. Her heart was pounding rapidly in her chest. She stared at him. She had never seen such emotion from him before. It was unsettling.

"My family – they'll get it in time. That we belong together. My mother will approve. You just have to give me more time." He was pleading now, his voice an octave higher than normal. "You have to let me work on them."

"I don't want you to work on them," Stacey whispered. "Tony, I don't want to marry you. I think I should go, actually."

She turned to head to her room. Her mind was spinning. She planned to pack a few things in a suitcase and go over to Allison's. She would get through the wedding and get back home. Seeing Tony like this was only an indicator of his true nature. Stacey had never seen it before. But now that she had, she knew she had to get out of here.

Tony's hand snapped out and reached for Stacey's. He was pulling her toward him. She tried to dig her feet against the floor but it was tile and made no difference.

He wrapped his arms around her and crushed her in a hug.

"Stacey," he whispered, "Stacey, you can't go. I've done all of this for you. Don't you see? All of this was for you. I tried to help you with your grandmother. I tried to help you with the job. From the first time I saw you on the yacht, I knew that I had to have you."

Muffled against his shirt, Stacey said, "You can't own people. They aren't yours to have." She pushed herself away from him. "Jesus, Tony! What is wrong with you?"

"Stacey, you're the first woman that I've felt this for. Don't you get it? All the others – they've meant nothing. They were all nothing. But you and I – I can feel what we have between us. I know you can feel it too! You're just confused."

"I'm not confused. Tony, I'm sorry. I didn't mean to upset you. Truly, I didn't. I'm sorry. I really like you. I do. From the very start. But it just isn't enough. I've been sitting in this villa like I'm in a dream or something. I have to get back to reality. I can't keep doing this." She gestured at the room and hoped it would make sense to him.

"I'll give you whatever you want," Tony pleaded. "Whatever you want. Diamonds. Furs. This island."

"It isn't about things," Stacey said, feeling sad. "It's about that connection. How I feel."

Tony looked stumped. In that moment, Stacey felt nothing but pity for him. He loved her. She knew that. But he also thought loving someone meant owning them. He thought it meant buying them whatever they wanted and allowing them to run away from their problems.

But Stacey didn't want gifts. She didn't want someone who was okay with her hiding out because she couldn't deal with her grandmother's death. She needed someone who would hold her up and push her forward. Make her do things she was struggling to do because it was good for her, not because it was easy.

"Tony, I'm going to go over to my sister's place, alright?" Her voice was soft in an attempt to soothe his ire.

"Stacey, marry me. Tonight. We'll leave the island. Forget about my family. They'll come around."

She shook her head. "No, Tony. Not only because it wouldn't be fair of me to do that to you, but also because you want your family to love who you love, too. And that isn't me. You'd regret it in time. Our similarities are nice. But that's not enough to make a foundation for a relationship, either."

She turned and left the room. Tony didn't come after her which was a relief. Stacey was unnerved by how passionate he was being. She knew that he cared about her, but she hadn't quite understood how deeply until now.

I should have seen it coming. I should have known he was falling too deep, she thought as she opened her suitcase. Stacey knew that she shouldn't blame herself for Tony's feelings. She couldn't control how he felt. But she had assumed they had merely liked each other. She hadn't known he loved her or was thinking about marriage. The thought made her head spin. Talk about too much too soon.

Stacey felt wrong taking anything he had gifted her while she had been here. Not after she had just told him she didn't want anything from him.

Stacey finished packing her suitcase with everything she had brought with her to the island. There was a door in her room that led directly to the beach. She decided she would cut across the beach to get to her sister.

With one last look at the room, Stacey turned around and left. She shut the door quietly behind her. She walked toward the beach as if it had a pull on her. The sand squished in between her toes. The stars were sparkling above her head. The surf crashed against her feet.

Stacey looked back at the villa. All the lights were off. She wasn't sure what Tony was thinking or doing. Her shoulders hurt where he had dug his thumbs into her skin. It had been scary to see him like that. If he was like that over his feelings for her, what would stop Tony from getting that way about other things?

She shivered, and not from the ocean breeze. Then Stacey picked up her suitcase and walked across the beach toward Allison's villa. It came into view in a matter of minutes and was lit up like a Christmas tree. Some of the other villas were illuminated as well. Guests had been arriving all day.

Stacey went over to Allison's bedroom window. She hoped Jacob wasn't in there. She put her head against the glass and rapped on it three times. Nothing. Stacey really didn't want to go through the front door. It was probably swarming with well-wishers and she didn't feel like talking right now.

Stacey was about to tap on the window again when Allison's face popped up. She frowned.

"What the hell are you doing?" she said through the window.

"Can you let me in? Through the bedroom door?"

"Yeah, sure."

Stacey backed away from the window and went over to the bedroom door that opened to the beach. Allison closed it behind her. She was dressed to impress tonight in a shiny purple dress. Her eyes were lined with gold that looked beautiful against her dark skin.

"Wow, you look beautiful," Stacey breathed.

Allison pointed to the suitcase. "What did you do? You couldn't have waited until after the wedding to dump him?"

Before Stacey could stop herself, she launched into the entire story about what had happened. Allison listened with avid interest. When she finished, her sister shook her head.

"Alright, well, he sounds like a fucking weirdo."

"He isn't."

"Why are you defending him? Wait. Don't tell me. Guilt. Fuck that. His reaction was really fucking weird."

Normally, Allison's crass mouth bothered Stacey. Tonight, however, there was something comforting about it.

She went on. "Wanting to get approval like that is old school. Also, his family is never going to like you. They never even gave you a shot. His reaction about wanting you and owning you – creepy."

Something in Stacey's face must have shown conflict because Allison sat down at the edge of the bed. She tugged on Stacey's arm until she was sitting down next to her.

"You fucked up," Allison said simply. "Everyone does it. You got caught up in Tony because he represented what you thought was a way out. You did like him, but he loved you. You can't stay with that imbalance."

"What about Jacob and you?" Stacey asked before she could stop herself.

"Jacob and I are more of a marriage that works out on both sides."

"What do you mean?"

"His money is appealing, right? And Jacob wants to marry someone and start popping out heirs to his fortune. It works out for both of us. He knows I won't be going behind his back to scheme and plot against him. And I get access to his money."

"Scheme and plot? He owns a tea company. Not exactly high stakes stuff," Stacey remarked.

"Hey, there are some serious assholes working in the tea business, alright?" Allison said with a smile.

"So, let me get this straight. He likes you because you have no connections that can mess him over. You're safe, basically. That doesn't bother you that he thinks of you like that?"

"No. It isn't as if I think of him as the love of my life."

"And this doesn't bother you?"

"Stacey, this is what I've wanted. I've looked for this. I know you think it's stupid and you disagree with it. But I want that money. I want that security that I am never going to get on my own. So I'm going to get it this way. And I'm fine with it. Not every marriage is about love. This one is more of a mutual understanding."

"I guess I just have a hard time wrapping my head around it."

"Well, don't. It isn't your problem. No offense, but you pretty much lost your fucking mind when Tina died. You've been living on an island shacking up with some guy that, for reasons beyond me, is in love with you to the point he just thinks if he buys you a lot of shit you'll feel the same way."

"Don't remind me. I feel awful."

"Well, stop feeling bad for yourself. You woke up now. You're going to go back home after the wedding and get your life together on your own terms." Allison stood up. "I have actual guests I need to go talk to. I have to intervene before Jacob literally bores them to death and we have to clean up the corpses."

She turned around to leave when Stacey spoke up, "Allison."

Her sister paused and looked over her shoulder.

"Thanks."

"I'm not as dumb as I look."

"Well, you aren't very good at math."

"Shut up," Allison said, but her tone was light and she was smiling.

For the first time in three months, Stacey felt a little bit of relief bloom in her chest.

Chapter Eight

Jacob actually looked nervous. It was a strange sight for Stacey. She was watching him struggle with his tie. Allison was already at the hall, getting ready in one of the rooms there for the wedding. Yet in all of the insanity, she had somehow forgotten her shoes. Stacey had gone to fetch them.

She hadn't been expecting to see Jacob here. Not only that, but he was alone. Stacey had been expecting a group of people to be floating around him, helping him. But he was struggling with his tie on his own in the middle of the foyer.

Stacey cleared her throat. Jacob almost jumped fifty feet in the air, then looked over at her.

"Sorry," she said. "Allison forgot her shoes."

"It's fine," he said, turning back to the mirror.

She watched his fingers stumble over the tie. Stacey was confident that Jacob knew how to tie a tie properly. To see him nervous was startling. From what she had learned yesterday, Jacob was marrying her sister because it made the most business sense, not because he loved her.

Stacey walked over to him. "Want some help?"

He let out a little groan of frustration and then nodded, turning to face Stacey. She went up to him. Her fingers curled around his tie. She had never been this close to Jacob before. Up close, she still couldn't understand how her sister was going to marry this guy. Billionaire or not, Stacey could only ever see herself marrying for love. To marry him for money just wasn't enough. His skin was so pale today that he was practically transparent. His eyes looked watery, as if he were allergic to something.

"Nervous?" she asked, trying to make conversation.

"Yes. Is Allison?"

Stacey's mind flicked back to Allison only ten minutes ago. Her sister had looked radiant in her gown. Her make-up was flawless. She was glowing in diamond jewelry. There were no nerves in Allison's face. This was what she had wanted, after all. She wasn't going to get jumpy about it now.

But one look at Jacob showed he was clearly nervous. Stacey took pity on him.

"Yes, she is."

He exhaled slowly. "It all happened so quickly."

"There," Stacey said, taking a step back to look at the tie.

Jacob turned back to the mirror and gave a curt nod. "Thank you."

"Not going to leave my sister at the altar, are you?" It was a joke but there was a hitch at the end of her question that made it sound serious.

Jacob shook his head. "No. Definitely not. Just nervous. You know, we were going to wait a little longer, originally. I thought if perhaps she wanted more time… after your grandmother passed."

Stacey didn't know this. Allison had made it sound as if they had jointly wanted it to unfold this quickly.

"Did she say why she wanted to move it up?"

"No, but I just assumed it was her own way of grieving over Tina. She was destroyed when it happened. I think focusing on the wedding helped her process it."

Was that healthier than what Stacey had done? Probably. Stacey had always prided herself on keeping her shit together but doing that after Tina died had been the last thing she had managed to accomplish. How had the tables turned to where Allison was the one who had herself together and not Stacey!

"Listen, I know what you are thinking," Jacob said suddenly.

"What?"

"How quickly it's moving. I know you're seeing Tony, so you at least understand how important business is in our lives."

Stacey didn't bother telling him that she had broken up with Tony. The whole thing still felt too messy to say aloud to someone other than Allison.

Jacob went on. "I don't know if Allison told you that my father is ill. He doesn't have much time left."

"Oh God, I'm sorry," Stacey replied, stricken.

"The control of the company is going to come to me. It is a big responsibility. Not only do I want someone that I can have children with so that the company can stay in the family, but I don't want to be alone either, going through the next few years." He shrugged and looked away from her.

Stacey got the sense that Jacob opening up was a rarity. All she had ever heard from him was a pompous attitude and long, dull stories. This was the first time she saw a real person underneath it all. Not wanting to be alone was something that she could relate to.

"Yeah, I get it," Stacey finally said. "Allison doesn't want to be alone either."

"People have been talking. About her and me, I mean. That she isn't my usual type. That she is just using me for my money. But your sister and I know what we both want out of this and it works out for both of us."

"Like a business deal."

"In a way. Anyway, I'm glad you're here to help her with her nerves."

"Well, I'm going to grab her shoes before she kills me," Stacey said lightly.

"I should get down there as well."

"Do you have anyone going with you?"

"No," Jacob said curtly before turning around.

There was something sad about that, Stacey thought as he nodded at her and left through the front door. She assumed people would be swarming around him. But for the front he put on, Stacey had seen that he was lonely and unsure of himself.

Stacey still didn't quite agree with Allison's way of doing things. Her entire goal had been to marry rich. Now that she was finally accomplishing it, would life be exactly how she had wished it to be? To help Jacob through his father's death, give him children and raise a family with him and be a life boat in the seas of his business struggles – Stacey couldn't picture Allison doing that.

To be fair, Stacey hadn't been able to picture herself losing her mind after Tina's death and hiding out here with Tony. So everyone was full of surprises lately.

<<◇>>

With no one to walk Allison down the aisle, she had asked if Stacey would do it. It made the most sense. Allison didn't want someone she hardly knew to walk her. Stacey was the only family around.

It was surreal for Stacey. Her sister glowed next to her like a diamond. Stacey had never seen a more beautiful bride. As they walked together, the crowd hushed, Stacey wondered what it would feel like if she were ever to get married. Surely, it wouldn't be as luxurious as this. Maybe something small and quiet with a handful of people. Her sister could return the favor with walking her down the aisle. She could almost picture it... except for the groom.

At first, Stacey thought she was imagining it. She had been focused on Jacob, who was waiting nervously at the altar. But no, there he was. Charlie was looking at her from one of the seats. Stacey hadn't known that he had been invited. His eyes were resting on her, not Allison.

The sight of him brought back a rush of memories. Their first date by the ocean. Their first kiss. Adele waiting in the lobby. Breaking up with him. Thinking that he was the one who had paid for Tina's nursing home stay. And ultimately, that day at her grandmother's funeral, where he had wanted to give her another chance and she had run away, too afraid to act on her feelings.

She dragged her eyes away from him. This was Allison's wedding. Stacey wasn't going to let herself get distracted by Charlie. They reached the altar. Stacey went to stand off to one side.

Awkwardly, Stacey found herself looking across the aisle at Tony. Jacob must have snagged him as best man at the last minute. Tony was staring at her. His face was like stone. There was no sign of the passionate side of him that she had seen the other night.

She avoided his gaze and turned to watch Jacob and Allison recite their vows. When they finished and leaned in for the kiss, Stacey could only shake her head a little. Her sister had achieved her 'goal,' no matter how silly Stacey thought it was. She married a man who wanted someone to support him during rough times ahead. They both knew it wasn't a marriage based on love, but of mutual caring and understanding, maybe even convenience.

That might work for Allison but it isn't what I want, Stacey thought as she watched the two kiss.

And in spite of her best intentions, she found herself looking over at Charlie once again.

Chapter Nine

Stacey had never seen a wedding reception quite like this before. Tents had been put up on the beach for the reception with room for dancing afterward. Some people lounged on the beach while others even swam. The moon was high up in the sky. The tents were covered in small fairy lights. It was a paradise.

Stacey was standing just outside one of the smaller tents. In front of her, people crowded the dance floor. Allison was in the middle of it. Jacob was spinning her around. Her dress was puffed out and swirling with her. The gems on it shimmered under the low lighting. She looked like a star that had crashed on the island.

A couple of times, Stacey had run into members of Tony's family. They regarded her with a cool indifference. She wondered if he had told them about the breakup. It was impossible to tell with their blank faces. She hadn't seen Tony since the wedding ceremony.

A breeze rolled in off the ocean. Stacey turned to look at it. The waters were dark. The stars reflected off of it, distorted by the waves. She walked away from the tent and headed toward the ocean. There were some people there in small clusters, drinking and laughing loudly.

She slipped her shoes off and let the water touch her feet. It was cold and caused her to shiver when it first rolled over her skin.

"I was going to go swimming, but it ended up being a bit too chilly for my liking."

Stacey froze. She didn't have to turn around to know who was behind her. Charlie walked up next to her and looked out at the ocean. He took in a deep breath and closed his eyes.

"I don't know how you could have stayed here for so long," he said.

"Why?"

"So lonely. I'm not a huge fan of islands. I feel disconnected from everything. Like I'm bobbing around in a giant bathtub." He still hadn't looked at her.

"You know, it's funny you say that. I've thought that before too. All the water in between the next city. It is lonely. Isolating."

"Is that why you're going home?"

"I see you've been talking to Allison."

"Yeah, we've had a little time to talk."

"Is that how you knew I've been staying here?"

Charlie chuckled. "No. No, Tony told me when we ran into each other a couple of months ago. He made sure to slide it in there for me to hear. Which I didn't mind. You just vanished after Tina's funeral. At least you were safely on some island instead of being sad somewhere else."

"Yeah. I guess so."

"Stacey –"

At the same time, she had said, "Charlie –"

The two of them laughed and Charlie ran his fingers through his hair. "Sorry. You go first."

"No, it's okay. You go."

The two of them stared at each other, at a standstill. Stacey had wanted to apologize for how she had acted at Tina's funeral. The words were bubbling in her mouth, waiting to spill out. She wanted to reach out and touch him and tell him that she had fucked things up. She should have gone with him and taken that chance.

But before either of them could say a word, another voice spoke up.

"Get away from her."

Surprised, Stacey looked over to see Tony barreling toward the two of them. His face was contorted with anger and he had his fists clenched. Alarmed, Stacey looked over at Charlie who was positioning himself in front of her.

"Tony, man, why don't you settle down?"

She hadn't smelled it at first due to the breeze from the ocean. But now that Tony was close enough, Stacey could smell the wafts of alcohol rolling off of him. He wasn't just a little drunk. He was completely intoxicated.

"Why don't we go back to that tent over there and talk this through?" Charlie said.

But Tony never replied. Instead, he swung at him. His fist connected with Charlie and sent him tumbling into the sand. A wave promptly rolled over his head which caused him to sputter up water.

"What are you doing?!" Stacey shrieked, alarmed.

Tony grabbed Charlie by the collar of his shirt, getting ready to deck him again. Stacey threw herself against him. The sudden collision threw him off balance. Already drunk, he lost his footing and landed in the sand next to Charlie.

Stacey helped Charlie get to his feet. Tony was slurring drunkenly as a wave rolled in over his head.

"Help me get him up before he drowns or something," Charlie said, rubbing his jaw.

Naturally, a crowd had formed. The sight of usually well composed Tony, drunk as a skunk and punching someone, had generated a lot of interest. Charlie was trying to prop Tony up to get him out of the water. Tony tried to push him off.

It was then that her sister burst through the crowd. She was staring at the three of them. Jacob was hurrying over. Tony pushed Charlie off again and slumped back down in the water.

"I got him," Jacob said to the two of them.

Allison hurried over to them. Stacey was alarmed at the fact that her wedding dress was getting wet, but she didn't seem to notice.

"What the hell happened?"

"Tony's drunk and just punched Charlie."

Charlie's face was already swelling. It had been a good punch. Even in the darkness, she could see his cheek was cut open.

"I'll get him patched up," Stacey said, grabbing his arm. "Allison, I am so sorry."

"What? Why? Tony losing his shit and punching people over you? I never would have pegged that happening. Over me, maybe. Not you." She was teasing her, Stacey realized with relief. She wasn't angry. "Anyway, go get him looked after."

Stacey nodded and grabbed Charlie's arm. She pulled him away from the beach before Tony could wriggle free of Jacob's grip and come after him. They cut through one of the larger tents. This one had a bartender who was busy serving drinks. Stacey tugged Charlie along until she felt him resist.

She turned to look at him. "What?"

"Come on. I want a drink. Whiskey or something."

"You're bleeding."

"It'll help with the pain." He grinned.

Stacey tried to protest but he weaved through the crowd toward the bar. He leaned forward, saying something to the bartender. She watched him and tried to ignore the way her heart was fluttering in her chest. The fairy lights that were looped around the top of the tent seemed to make him glow. It was as if he was the brightest spot in the entire area.

She looked away and told herself to get a grip. After what she had done to Charlie, she didn't deserve another chance with him. She shouldn't even think about it. Not only that, but now Tony had punched him in the face. Wonderful. Why even go near him at this point?

Charlie came back holding a glass of whiskey. He took a swig and winked at her over the rim of the glass. Stacey turned away quickly before her face could betray her thoughts.

"Where are you marching off to? You don't even know which villa is mine," he pointed out.

Stacey slowed down so he could catch up. They were leaving the tent now. Ahead of them were the guest villas. Most were dark. There were a few stragglers here. At one point, their hands brushed against each other. The touch was electric. It felt as if it rocked her to her center, and it was only their hands touching. She felt like a schoolgirl with a crush.

"Here," he said, stopping in front of one of the smaller ones.

A thought struck her out of the blue. "Adele isn't here."

"Ah, yes. That's right," Charlie replied as he opened the front door.

"Why?" Stacey pressed, even though technically it wasn't any of her business.

They stepped into the living room. Stacey had never been in the smaller villas before. She recalled Tony telling her they were the oldest and not used much. He liked bringing big groups to the island, so he had stopped building the smaller homes.

Charlie looked over her shoulder. "Is that any of your concern?"

Stacey felt struck and stammered out, "N-no! It isn't. I'm sorry."

Charlie let out a loud laugh and then winced, gingerly touching his cheek. "Shit. Ow."

"There's a first aid kit in the bathroom. Each place has one," Stacey said as she headed toward the bathroom.

"How thoughtful." His tone was dry.

"Why were you laughing at me?" she asked as she rummaged through the cabinet.

"Because you thought I was being serious about asking about Adele," Charlie said.

She found the kit and pulled it out. Then she pointed to the edge of the tub.

"Yes, nurse," he replied, sitting down on it.

Stacey tilted his face to one side so she could see where Charlie had been punched. His skin was warm under her fingertips. She could feel her own pulse in her fingertips. It was racing. She wondered if he could feel it.

Underneath Charlie's eye was a small gash. She could tell that he luckily wouldn't need stitches.

"I think his ring got you," she mumbled as she looked through the kit.

"Probably. Thought I saw some big shiny thing on his finger." He wrinkled his noise.

"I'm going to clean it up first. You're probably going to end up with a black eye."

Charlie smirked. "I'll look tough, right?"

Stacey rolled her eyes. "This is going to sting."

"I can handle it," he boasted and then cursed when Stacey started to clean it. "Fuck. That hurts."

"Big tough guy, huh?" Stacey quipped.

He laughed. His breath brushed against her cheek. Stacey tried to ignore how close she was to him. As she cleaned up his cut, she refused to look into his eyes. Charlie shifted a little on the edge of the tub.

"I'm not seeing Adele."

"Oh?" She tried to keep her voice neutral.

"It was stupid. I thought – after you left… at the time, it made sense. It was easier just caving to what my dad wanted. For a while, I figured I'd marry her. It would stop all the plotting and planning from my dad and my brother, Eric. Peace and quiet."

"And?"

"I couldn't do it. No matter how hard I tried to tell myself that Adele could work for me, she wasn't you."

Stacey felt her breath catch but she refused to let herself get distracted. She refused to let herself hope, even for a moment, that Charlie would want anything to do with her.

"Why did he punch me?" Charlie said abruptly, changing the subject.

"I don't know," she lied. "Drunk, I guess." It was easier to lie than admit that he had known that she still loved Charlie.

Charlie grabbed her hand. She let out a small gasp, startled.

"Hey," she chastised, "you're lucky I just applied the bandage. You would have messed it up."

Charlie didn't reply. He held her hand gently. Unlike when Tony had grabbed her, she could break free at any time. But Stacey didn't want to break free. Instead, she watched as he pressed his lips against her fingertips. His eyes were on hers.

"When I left Adele, I thought I could win you back. But then I heard from Jacob about Tina dying. I could only imagine your grief. Your anger at how things had turned out." Each word he said gently brushed against her fingers, sending shivers through her. "I could picture a storm inside of you. I had to see you. I thought – I shouldn't have approached you at the funeral like that. It wasn't fair of me."

"What? No, I shouldn't have – I was so stupid that day, Charlie. I should have opened up to you and really listened. But I was so afraid –"

"I should have waited. Instead of trying to convince you to be with me, I should have been there to support you. Maybe if I had, you wouldn't have…"

"What? Run away? I still would have. I was too afraid to let you in. I took the coward's way out. I let myself succumb to my grief and I just didn't want to deal with anything anymore. Allison was right. I lost myself through who I was seeing."

Charlie kissed her fingertips so softly that Stacey thought she could be imagining it. Distantly, she could hear music from the reception. It was the only thing she could hear over the sound of her beating heart.

"You're back now though, aren't you?" he whispered. "You're awake."

"I'm awake," she breathed.

He pulled her toward him. His lips touched hers. The touch was like waking up from a nightmare. The last three months, which had been a fog of hiding her emotions and ignoring reality, seemed to dissipate when Charlie kissed her.

The kiss was gentle and full of longing. There were a lot unspoken words there. Things still needed to be discussed. But for right now, feeling Charlie kiss her like this was more than Stacey had ever wanted in her life.

He broke away from her and said very gently, "Come home, Stacey."

So she did.

Chapter Ten

Seasons were non-existent on Tony's island. It was in a permanent state of constant summer. When Stacey stepped out of the cab to look at her apartment complex for the first time in three months, she was startled to see that it was well into autumn in the city.

The leaves were changing color. One of the trees nearby was already bare. There were no summer storms on the horizon. There was a hint of chill to the wind, as if winter was quietly promising to arrive.

The cab drive home had shown her a lot of construction. Charlie's company was remodeling and rebuilding a lot of the buildings that had fallen into disrepair. The public library was covered in construction signs. There was a park being built where there had once been a junk yard. It was exciting to see positive changes being made to her area of town.

She had also noticed how many people were trying to sell their homes. Everyone was trying to cash in on the remodeling of this section of the city. The sellers were probably hoping to interest someone from a major company like Charlie's in buying their homes and flipping them. Change had steam-rolled in while Stacey had been hiding out.

She opened the door to the lobby and was taken aback. The tile that had once been cracked in places had been repaired. It was jarring. Nothing else seemed to have been fixed down here. But the mere fact that at least that much was accomplished meant the owners of the building were finally starting to fix things.

Stacey climbed the steps. She was oddly nervous about going into her old apartment. She got to her floor and practically ran into Leon. At first she didn't recognize him. He had gotten so tall in the last few months. He had a cigarette dangling from his mouth and was holding a cheap-looking phone in the other hand.

"Holy shit! Stacey!"

"You shouldn't curse like that, Leon," Stacey said automatically.

He let out a loud laugh, "Look at you! Gone for what, four months, and still ready to lecture."

"Three months, actually."

"Everyone was waiting for the apartment to go up for rent or something."

"Nah. I'm back now."

"What about your sister? She's a babe."

"She's a bit too old for you, Leon," Stacey remarked. "Also, she's married."

"Ah, really? Damn. Born a little too early to snag a woman like her," he said wistfully and then looked serious. "I'm sorry about your grandmother. My mom wanted to come by and see if you needed anything. Any help. But you were gone."

"Yeah, I sorta left in a hurry," Stacey replied, feeling guilty.

"Well, you're back now. The building was sold when you were gone. We got new landlords."

"Is that why the tile downstairs is repaired?"

"You noticed that? Yeah, pretty amazing. Anyway, I should go. I have a girlfriend now and don't wanna piss her off. See you around."

Leon moved past her. Stacey watched him leave, marveling again at how tall he was. She wondered who had bought the building. At least they weren't trying to kick anyone out.

Stacey stopped in front of her apartment and unlocked the front door. With a deep breath, she opened it and stepped inside.

Nothing had changed visually, of course. Everything was right where Stacey had left it when she had run away. She stood there, almost afraid to take another step. The dam she had placed around her heart was threatening to crack and let everything she had been holding in free.

Stacey walked into the living room. Everything had a layer of dust over it. She was going to clean the entire place out, she thought idly as she ran her fingers over the coffee table.

She could feel it pulling her. Some sort of force propelling her to what had been Tina's room. Even if Stacey could stop it, she wouldn't. She needed to do this. Her breath caught in her throat. The dam shook violently in her heart. Stacey stopped in front of the door. It was firmly shut. She must have done that. She couldn't remember closing it.

Stacey pushed open Tina's door and looked inside. The bed was a little messy from when they had packed her things up for the nursing home. It had hurt to take her there. But Stacey had thought she was going to have more time.

She stepped inside the room and let the full force of it finally hit her in the face. Tina's loss, still too fresh for Stacey, rolled over her. The dam broke inside of her. Her legs went weak and she sunk to the floor.

For the first time since her grandmother died, Stacey allowed herself to finally grieve. She stayed there on the floor for a long time, sobbing her eyes out, letting herself feel engulfed by the loss.

Stacey had been trying to sleep. She had felt exhausted after crying for so long. She was jet-lagged from the trip. It had made perfect sense to go to bed early. But lying there in bed felt suffocating. She could feel how alone she was. This was one of the things that Stacey had been trying to outrun. The lonely feeling that filled the apartment was enough to make her want to cry again.

Stacey looked at the clock. It was only seven at night. She sat up, deciding not to spend another second in bed. Sleep just wasn't going to happen, and all she was going to do was drive herself crazy.

Charlie had texted her once she had landed, saying that he was happy that she was back home. He had gone up north for a business trip directly after the wedding. Talking things out with him would have to wait until he came back. Nothing else had happened that night, but still, the kiss they had shared in the bathroom had been filled with promise. Stacey was eager to see where that was going to go.

She liked to think that she was going to get another shot with Charlie. Stacey was ready to put her heart on the line and work through the differences in their lives to try again. She had been too quick to break up with him in the first place. If only she had stayed with him, perhaps things would be completely different now.

Her phone went off, breaking her out of her thoughts about Charlie. Stacey looked at it and was surprised to see it was her old boss, William. Dimly, she could recall him back at the funeral. He had been telling her about something. She struggled to remember. Something about a new business, maybe? It was hard to remember anything from Tina's funeral. It was like one hazy bad dream.

"Hello?"

"So, it is true! I can't believe it!" William's booming voice came through the other line. "Allison told me you were back in town, but I thought she was pulling my leg."

"Allison contacted you?" Stacey asked, surprised because she knew Allison and Jacob were on their honeymoon somewhere in Europe.

"Yup. Said you were looking for a job."

"Oh. Yeah. I am, actually." There was no way she was going to ask Tony if she could still work at the office after they had broken up.

"Come meet me at the deli down the street from your apartment."

"Sure. I'll be there soon."

Stacey changed quickly and made sure she looked decent. She knew she probably looked a little rough, but it was nothing that William hadn't seen before. Back when the restaurant had been busy, Stacey had usually looked terrible.

When she walked into the deli, she looked around for him. Someone waved her over. To her surprise, it was Amanda. She hadn't seen Amanda in quite some time. Next to her was Brad. It was nice to see that the two of them were still together. She walked over to their table.

"William call you guys too?" Stacey asked after giving Amanda a hug.

"Not really. We already work for him," Amanda replied as Stacey sat down.

"Really?"

"Yup. I only started a couple of weeks ago. I left the job I had taken when the restaurant closed. William said he'd fit better into my school schedule."

Stacey looked over at Brad, who shrugged. "I needed a job."

"Where is he, anyway?" she asked the two of them, looking around.

"Right here."

Someone had stopped in front of their table. He was holding two coffees. Stacey blinked.

"William?" she asked in surprise.

"I know, I know. I lost a lot of weight."

It was true. William, who had once been the largest man Stacey had known, was now slim. He looked away from her, almost bashful at his progress.

"Wow, that is amazing. What brought that on?" she asked as he sat down next to her.

"Boredom. Losing the restaurant meant I had a lot of free time on my hands. Which sounded great at first. It was nice not worrying about the day-to-day things. But I got bored. My wife – she started talking about going out for walks and things like that to keep me from getting restless. I just started losing weight the more I worked out.”

“Well, that’s great, really,” Stacey replied.

“What about you? Last time we saw you was at Tina’s funeral,” William said.

“I am still so sorry about what happened with her,” Amanda spoke up.

“Thanks, guys. Yeah, I just got back into town. I sort of took off for a while.”

“Hid out,” Amanda quipped but she smiled gently at Stacey.

“Yeah. I guess I lost my shit there for a little bit,” she admitted.

“I’ve lost my shit more times than I can count,” Brad said.

“Well, I’m back now. And ready to hear what you wanted to see me about,” Stacey said to William.

“Right. Well,” he cleared his throat, “all those times I was out jogging or whatever, I noticed all the renovations going on in the city. And I saw a lot of building owners that were trying to sell their places. They knew companies like Charlie’s were interested in remodeling the city or cutting deals with private places to remodel. Over the last few months, I saw that everyone was trying to sell but there weren’t a lot of takers.”

"So, you want to hop in on it," Stacey finished. "Buy up some of the cheaper places and flip them. Turn a profit."

"We already own one residence," Amanda said.

It clicked in Stacey's head. "You bought the apartment where I live."

William smiled. "Figured it'd be a good place to start. The landlords there didn't seem keen on the place. They had been banking on Charlie's construction company to buy it up. When he changed to remodeling public buildings and parks, they were pretty bitter. It left them wide open for me to swoop in and buy it up."

"So, what? You're going to improve it – hopefully you aren't going to kick anyone out."

"No, of course not. But the top floor of your complex is what… empty?"

"Yeah. Because it fell into such disrepair – oh. I get it now. You're going to rent them out for a higher price. Elite apartments on the top floor."

"Right," William said, rubbing his hands together. "And if it works, we can start doing that all around the city. There is a market there. We just need to grab it."

"Okay. Sounds like a good idea. But what would I be doing?"

"You'd be my assistant, of course. Come with me to any meetings. Help me scope out the properties. I have Amanda working on the paperwork side of things.

Dealing with the city. Making sure the deal is clean. I have Brad as…" he trailed off, as if unsure why exactly Brad was there.

"Amanda's assistant," Brad said.

"Sure," William replied slowly. "Amanda's assistant, I guess."

"Well, that sounds great," Stacey said. "Perfect timing, really."

"Great! I'm so happy. It is like the gang is back together. Minus everyone at the restaurant I didn't care about. Let's work out the details," William said, pulling out a folder.

Stacey leaned forward, interested. It was nice knowing that she was going to be doing something on her own. It felt like a fresh start.

Chapter Eleven

Stacey had papers strewn out in front of her. She was looking them over. William had given them to her a few days ago to review. It was a business plan of sorts. This was her third time going over them. It wasn't that she didn't trust William. It was mostly that he hadn't done a fantastic job with the restaurant. She wanted to make sure everything was in place. Perhaps this is where William's talents really were, instead of the restaurant business.

A knock on her door snapped her out of focus. She wondered who it could be. Allison wasn't due back from her honeymoon for another week. Stacey opened the door.

Charlie stood in front of her. He had a suitcase by his feet as if he had just arrived from the airport. He smiled at her.

"Hey," was all he said but it was enough.

Before Stacey could overthink it, she swung her arms around Charlie's and pressed her lips against his. For a spilt second, he didn't do anything. She wondered if he was going to push her away.

But then his hands wrapped around her. They stumbled into her apartment. Stacey almost lost her footing, but Charlie had a firm grip around her waist. She felt winded, as if she had run a marathon. The sight and feel of him was enough to make her feel dizzy.

He smiled against her lips. "Wait, wait."

"What?" she mumbled, dazed.

He turned around and pulled his suitcase in from the hallway and closed the door. Then Charlie turned back around and pulled her toward him. Their lips met again. Stacey could feel his heart hammering underneath her fingertips as she pressed her hands against his chest. She could feel his muscles underneath. She could feel his stubble scratching against her skin.

"Did you just get into town?" Stacey finally asked when she came back up for air.

"Yeah. But I wanted to see you before I did anything else." He smiled against her cheek before grazing his lips against hers.

The fact that he had come directly to see her made Stacey so happy that she could hardly contain it. She grabbed him by the hand and led him down the hallway toward her bedroom.

"It's a mess," she apologized as she opened the door.

Charlie wrapped his arms around her from behind and whispered, "I don't care."

His mouth left butterfly kisses down her neck. His hands slid down along her body.

"I want to taste you," he whispered in her ear.

Stacey felt her knees go weak. His breath against her neck and his hands along her body was too much. She turned around and practically dragged him to the bed. They collapsed as one onto the springy mattress in a heap.

Together, they fumbled with each other's clothes. Stacey wanted him urgently and she could tell that he was feeling the same way by the way he stripped her. When their bare skin touched, she gasped. His skin was warm against hers. She marveled at feeling him against her. She had thought this would never happen again.

His tongue licked her nipples gently before sucking on each, rolling her breasts around in his hands. Stacey closed her eyes and gave herself over to the sensations. Charlie's mouth was warm around her nipples as he cupped her breasts. Then he dragged his tongue in the middle of them as if he wanted to taste her skin.

He left a trail of kisses down her stomach toward her pussy, which was soaking wet. When his tongue finally probed her wet folds, Stacey let out a moan. Oh, she had missed this. She had missed Charlie's mouth down there, exploring her. He seemed to know exactly what she liked and how good it felt for her.

But Stacey wanted more. Coming out of her haze, she begged, "Let me taste you too."

Charlie moved away from her and lay down on the bed. Stacey got on top of him, moving so her pussy was near his face. He gripped her hips and pulled her pussy down onto his mouth, eating her hungrily. Stacey moaned in pleasure and gripped his cock. Stroking it gently, she moved her tongue up his shaft. It was pulsing in her hand and hard as a rock.

Stacey rolled her tongue along the tip as Charlie worked on her pussy. Waves of intense pleasure were rolling over her as she engulfed the tip of his dick with her mouth. She could hear a muffled moan from Charlie.

Stacey took more of him in her mouth. She liked how full her mouth felt and the sensation it gave her to fit as much of him as she could. She swirled her tongue around. Behind her, Charlie sucked gently on her clit before sliding a finger in her soaking wet pussy.

As her own pleasure mounted, she worked on Charlie's cock. She could feel his cock twitch in her mouth. His fingers wrapped in her hair and moved her head off of his dick.

"Not yet," he growled before his mouth went back on her pussy.

Her orgasm hit her. It was so intense that all she could do was go limp on his body as she quivered and shook. Her climax felt as if it was touching all parts of her, from her head down to her toes. The whole time, Charlie held onto her and rolled his tongue around her pussy.

When her orgasm stopped, he gently rolled her off of him and then slid on top of her. He bent down to kiss her. Stacey could taste herself on him. Then he was guiding his dick deep inside of her.

She had missed this. As he entered her, she pulled him close, looking into his eyes. Stacey had thought that she would never feel this again. She had assumed that she was never going to have sex like this again – where they knew each other so well that everything made perfect sense. Each movement was giving one another the highest amount of pleasure.

As he moved inside of her, Stacey clung to him as if he might suddenly vanish. She rocked her hips along with his movements. Charlie slid his arms under her back and brought her close. His thrusting picked up speed. He began to move urgently, letting out soft moans in her ear.

"Stacey," he grunted as he came close to his climax, "I love you."

The words took what little breath she had out of her. Stacey looked at him in surprise. Her pleasure was momentarily forgotten. All she could focus on was that she had finally heard the words she had hardly let herself dream about hearing. She smiled at him.

"I love you too," she whispered.

Charlie smiled and their lips met. This kiss was different. It was soft and full of promise. Then he moved inside of her and moaned. He was climaxing, Stacey realized, and she pulled him close. His

movements were enough to send her over the edge for a
second time.

Together, like always, they came. This was how it
was supposed to be, Stacey thought to herself as she
allowed herself to orgasm. She wanted to be linked with
Charlie in this way for the rest of her life.

Afterward, Charlie held her. She rested her head on
his chest and listened to his heart beating steadily. His
fingers trailed along her back. She could feel him
drawing patterns on her skin with the tips of his fingers
and it made her smile. She felt completely at peace.
How long had it been since she felt this way?

"So, tell me."

"Tell you what?" Stacey asked, peering up at him.

"The last three months. I'll tell you mine if you tell
me yours," he joked as his fingers stroked her hair.

"Not much to say, is there? I ran away. Easier not to
deal with how I was feeling about Tina than stick
around here. Tony offered a way out. I shouldn't have
taken it. It was stupid of me."

"Don't be so hard on yourself, Stacey. You had just
lost Tina. You were grieving. Scared and hurt. I don't
blame you for what you did."

"When you came to me and said that… well, when
you were talking about maybe giving us another chance
– I wanted that so much. More than anything. But I was

so afraid. I was so afraid of opening up and getting hurt. It was easier to run away with Tony because deep down, I think I knew I wasn't in any danger of ever loving him. Like I love you."

Charlie kissed the top of her head. The gesture was small but still made Stacey feel happy. There was something casual about it, as if they had been together forever, that she really enjoyed.

"When you ran off with him, I assumed that it was over and done with. I mean, how could I compete with that? Even though… it bothered me. I don't mean that you had chosen someone else. Mostly that you had chosen Tony. I wasn't sure if he was the best one for you."

"Why is that?" Stacey asked curiously.

Charlie gave a small shrug. "I've worked with him on and off throughout the years. I know what his family is like. I mean, don't get me wrong. Mine is fucked up. But so is his. He goes through all these different women trying to find one that would meet his mother's approval. It's really important to him that they approve of whomever he dates. So far, they never have."

"I thought I was really special, meeting his family," Stacey said with a laugh. "I thought it meant he was interested in me on a whole different level."

"Well, if it makes you feel better, I don't think I've ever seen him punch a man over someone he was dating."

Frowning at the memory, Stacey said, "He said that we were similar. That we both came from nothing and that I was trying to make my way. He wanted to help me. But all I did was let him make everything easier for me. I allowed him to help me with Tina. I allowed him to whisk me off to an island instead of dealing with how I was really feeling. Maybe we are similar. But I didn't want to be coddled like that."

"Did you tell him this?"

"Yeah. It didn't go well, trust me. I had never seen him like that before. He was so upset that I didn't love him in that way. He was… scary, actually."

Charlie's grip tightened around her. "Better now that you're away from him then. If Tony was like that then, who knows what would have come up if you had stayed with him."

Stacey shook her head. "I know. I don't know. I really messed things up."

"Tony has accomplished a ton in his life. He probably just wants someone to share it with."

"He'll find someone," Stacey said although she still felt guilty.

Charlie, sensing her mood, changed the subject. "Still can't believe your sister married Jacob."

"Yeah, that's a whole other thing. I don't get how she could marry someone she doesn't love. But he told me his dad is ill. Probably won't live long. So he wants someone by his side while he takes control of the company. He wants kids too, eventually. Allison is okay with all of this. Perfect… weird match made in heaven."

"So, you couldn't do what your sister did?"

"What?" Stacey shook her head. "No. Allison has always wanted that life. She hated being poor. She hated wanting things and not being able to get them. But I always thought marriage is about love. Nothing else."

Charlie tilted her face up to his. "That's why I love you," he said in all seriousness.

They kissed and when it ended, Stacey said, "Your family…"

He let out a playful groan. "What about them? You don't want to meet them, do you?"

"No, no, not yet. I was just curious why all you rich people have weird families."

Charlie laughed. "Boredom and money."

"Yeah, but surely, you guys could go travel," Stacey pointed out, "or take a class in something. Or literally do anything like fill a swimming pool with money."

"That seems unsanitary."

Stacey rolled her eyes and Charlie laughed. He kissed her again and then looked thoughtful.

"I don't know," he finally admitted. "My dad was pretty thrilled when I finally dated Adele. When I dumped her, he was pretty pissed off. He wants me to hire Eric and give him a high-ranking job in the company."

"Why don't you?"

"My brother is a real asshole," he said without any trace of humor.

"You've mentioned before that you two don't get along. But, surely, he has to accept the fact that the company is yours by now."

"He won't. He isn't nice. He isn't kind. He's all the negatives of my parents in one person. Maybe things would have been different if he had been born first and was trained in the company. But as the younger sibling, all he did was slack off and fool around. Now he wants to be taken seriously, and I'm not prepared to give him that. So he whines to our dad a lot."

"But you said your father had a stroke…"

"Yes. He gets worse with each passing day. I guess that's where Jacob and I are similar. Both of our fathers are dying."

"What happens when he passes away?"

"Insanity. Family coming out of the woodwork like vultures over a corpse, trying to suck up to me. Eric probably planning some stupid shit. The usual."

He sounded exhausted just talking about it. Stacey trailed her fingers along his jaw. He felt tense all over. The pleasure that Charlie had obviously been feeling before had drained from him. She felt bad that his family caused him such stress. She felt nervous at the idea of ever meeting them.

Charlie grabbed her hand and kissed her fingers. "But you're here. So I'll be okay."

"Your family won't like me, will they? I seem to be having bad luck with them."

"Fuck them. Even if they don't, I don't care. I want you and only you. I don't want them." Charlie said seriously.

It was so different from what Tony had wanted. He had wanted full acceptance of her from his family. But Charlie didn't care about that. The fact that he only wanted her made her happier than he could know.

When he brought her in for another kiss, Stacey couldn't believe how content she felt.

Chapter Twelve

Stacey watched as her sister made tea. She had spent five minutes telling Stacey that the tea leaves were from Jacob's own company. It apparently was going to be the best tea that Stacey would ever taste. The way Allison was pitching it, she wondered if Jacob should just let her sell the tea. She was bound to sell a ton.

"You make this sound as if it's some miracle elixir," Stacey finally said, cutting Allison off.

"Hey, it's amazing, alright."

Allison was holding a teapot that probably cost as much as Stacey's monthly rent. It was painted beautifully in bright red and green. The colors swirled together and formed the logo of Jacob's tea company. In the spotless kitchen, Allison stood out. She was wearing a pale pink dress with her hair swept up in a bun. She almost looked like a fifties housewife. It was a strange sight.

"Well, tell me about the honeymoon, at least."

Allison had come back into town yesterday. Stacey had been busy with William, going over things for his new real estate office, so she had missed the welcome back party that was thrown for the newly married couple. Secretly, Stacey was relieved. Allison had told her that Tony was coming, and she was keen on avoiding him.

"It was amazing. I mean, we toured most of Europe. The nice places, anyway."

"Ah, look at you. Sounding like a rich snob already," Stacey joked.

"I'll ignore that because I'm in a good mood. Jacob would stop by some of the offices and see how things were being run. I would explore, tour the city. Bought myself some trinkets."

"Like a new wardrobe?" Stacey asked, pointing to the new dress her sister was wearing.

"Naturally." She slid a cup on a fancy saucer toward Stacey. "Try it."

"It's just tea," Stacey protested.

Allison rolled her eyes. "That cup of tea costs more than you could ever wrap your head around."

"What is it with rich people paying insane prices for things that are really just the same stuff us regular people buy?"

"Because what else are they going to buy, Stacey? A thousand packets of tea or one box for the same price? It's all about the image. Selling a certain lifestyle."

Stacey looked down at her cup of tea, waiting for it to cool off a little. It was slightly purple, which was alarming. She realized she hadn't asked Allison what sort of tea this even was.

"So, now what for you?" she asked Allison.

"Goal achieved. I can relax now. Jacob is at the main office but he's talking about going to Hong Kong next week."

"I guess I won't be seeing you as much, huh?" Stacey asked and for some reason, felt oddly sad.

"Ah, sister. You're finally going to miss me."

"Maybe. I won't admit it though," Stacey said with a laugh. "With everything that has happened… you know, I have to say that I didn't think you would actually go through with marrying Jacob."

"I know. You thought I would suddenly change my mind. Decide to marry for love or whatever. But this is what I wanted. And I finally have it." She sighed happily.

"Yes, but he's so – he's so boring," Stacey whispered, even though Jacob wasn't home.

"He is, but only because of his social anxiety. He gets so nervous in front of groups of people."

"Jacob. We're talking about the same Jacob, right?" Stacey asked, having a hard time picturing this.

"Yes. That's why he talks so much. It was something he learned from his dad. Talk until you feel alright."

"Which is apparently never because he never stops talking."

"Yeah, true. But what can I do about it? I just let him ramble. Listen, I know he's boring everyone. I'm sure deep down he knows it as well. But I'm not about to tell him to stop what works for him. I just pretend that what he has to say is really interesting. Are you going to try the tea or not?"

Stacey had forgotten about the tea. She looked down at it. Little by little, she had been collecting information about Jacob. Perhaps he wasn't as bad as Stacey had assumed.

Allison went on, "I think we'll make a good team together. That's what really matters. You can have some passionate love affair with someone but once the zest fades away, then what? You're stuck with them."

"When did you become so jaded about love?"

"It isn't jaded."

"Sounds jaded to me. What if you find someone else while you're with Jacob?"

"Stacey, honestly." Allison sounded exasperated. "Stop worrying about my life. Focus on yours. Are you back with Charlie yet?"

"Yet? Were you just assuming we would get back together?"

"Yeah, of course. Besides, you have that look on your face."

"What look?"

"The look of getting laid by someone who knows what they are doing." She looked thoughtful. "You never had that look with Tony, now that I think about it."

Not wanting to discuss Tony any further, Stacey said quickly, "Yes, we're back together."

Allison rubbed her hands together as if this was a personal victory for her. "Fantastic. I knew it. That's great. Are you bringing him?"

"Bringing him where?"

"I didn't tell you?"

When Stacey shook her head, her sister said, "This weekend we're having a party. Small event. I promise. Just sort of a little party here for everyone who couldn't make it to the wedding."

"Wait. How many after-parties do you people need to celebrate your crazy marriage?" Stacey said, rolling her eyes.

"Ha ha, very funny," responded Allison, not looking very amused.

Not wanting to get into an argument with her sister, Stacey asked, "Who couldn't make it to the wedding? There were like two hundred people there."

"Some of his business associates and friends couldn't make it." Allison leaned forward. "Come on. You have to come."

"Why?"

"Because."

There was something in her sister's gaze – it was a vulnerability. Stacey hadn't seen that in a long time. Allison, normally confident, felt nervous at the idea of hosting a party as Jacob's wife for the first time. Stacey realized this was important to her.

"Yeah, of course. I'll be there. I'll bring Charlie too."

Allison smiled. "Great. Now, will you try the tea?"

Stacey picked up the tea and hesitantly took a sip. Maybe it was because it was purple or the fact that it was expensive as hell, but she was expecting it to taste weird. Instead, it seemed to explode in her mouth with a vibrant flavor she couldn't pinpoint. Her eyes widened slightly, and she swallowed.

"That is some good fucking tea," Stacey admitted, and Allison laughed.

"Told you," she said, turning away to pour herself a cup. "Stacey… you know if you need anything now, I can get it for you. A new place to live. Or whatever. Anything."

She was touched by Allison's offer. Stacey knew that her sister meant well. But after losing herself to the wealth that Tony had given her, she wasn't eager to fall back into that trap. She had managed to escape her own grief and fog back at that island and didn't want any more handouts.

Stacey gave a small shake of her head. "No, thanks," she replied, and she meant it.

"You look beautiful, honestly. Stop checking," Charlie said to Stacey as she double-checked her make-up in the compact mirror.

"Sorry. I still hate these sorts of gatherings."

"Allison is going to be there. I'm going to be there. It'll be nice."

It was the weekend of the little party at Allison and Jacob's place. Even though Stacey should be used to going to these events by now, she still felt nervous for some reason.

"Well, you seem nervous too," she pointed out. "You keep fidgeting."

It was true. Ever since Charlie had picked her up, he had been acting a little odd. He was friendly and nothing but a gentleman, but there seemed to be something else going on. She had pointed it out twice already, but he had brushed her off about it.

"I am not," he retorted, brushing her off for a third time.

Stacey rolled her eyes. "Whatever. Like you said, it's just Jacob. I'll be there. My sister will be there."

He smiled at her teasing. He looked incredibly handsome tonight, although Stacey was hard pressed to recall any time when he didn't look handsome. She was happy to be going to this event with him – to be with him in general.

It didn't take long to arrive at the party. They were taken up to the top floor, where Allison now lived. When they stepped inside, Stacey saw that her sister was true to her word. It seemed to be a small affair. There was a group in the middle which had formed around Jacob. He was telling a story in that typical slightly pompous manner of his. All traces of the man who had been nervous before his wedding had been erased.

Allison saw them first. She waved them over, weaving her way expertly through the small crowd, saying hello to people as she passed.

"She's good." Charlie pointed out as her sister shook the hand of a man three times her size.

"She's always been good with people," Stacey replied, thinking to herself that if anyone could be new to this world and navigate it with ease, it would be her sister.

"You're here!" Allison exclaimed when she got to them.

She brought Stacey in for a hug. At the same moment, Stacey commented, "Everything looks beautiful."

"Thanks. We're going to have snacks and everything served soon. You should go out on the balcony. It's amazing at night." She squeezed her hand and lowered her voice, "I'm really glad you're here."

"Me too."

"All right. I'll leave you two to it. I have to go say hello to George over there," Allison said, motioning her head in the direction of a sour-looking old man who just entered, "or he'll complain for forty years that I was rude to him."

Stacey watched Allison leave to go over to the man. Then she looked back at Charlie who laced his fingers through hers.

"Guess we should mingle," she said to him.

"Come on." He pulled her forward gently and together they walked into the gathering.

Stacey had lost track of Charlie thirty minutes ago. Last she had seen him, someone from Japan had cornered him to discuss construction. She had gone to the bathroom and hadn't seen him since. She had set off to look for him when Allison pulled her over to listen to a dull conversation between Jacob and the old man from earlier.

"Don't leave me alone with this man," she mumbled when she had dragged Stacey over. "He's rude and I want to slap him."

So Stacey stood dutifully by her sister's side. To be honest, she had tuned the conversation out. Social anxiety or not, Jacob was fantastic at droning on to fill any possible gaps in the conversation. George, the old man, was staring Jacob down and seemed very aggressive about tea. It would have been comical if it wasn't so dull.

She was about to tell Allison that she was going off to find Charlie when two more guests entered the party. Their arrival brought Stacey crashing out of her daze.

"No fucking way," she breathed.

George, who had been in the middle of a speech, looked over at her in surprise. "Excuse me?" he said coldly.

But Stacey ignored him. Allison saw instantly what she had seen and mumbled a curse word before excusing the two of them from the conversation.

"What are they doing here together?" Stacey whispered.

"I didn't invite either of them. Jacob must have."

The two sisters turned to watch as Tony and Adele entered the party, arms linked together.

Chapter Thirteen

"Well, makes sense they're dating, right? They both hate Charlie." Allison paused. "And you, I guess. Whatever, don't let it get to you. They can't do anything to you, you know that. If they do the smallest thing, I'll kick them out. They're probably just here to make you feel uncomfortable."

Stacey listened to Allison as she watched Tony and Adele stop to say hello to people. Adele looked as if she had stepped out of a glossy magazine. Tony had outdone himself tonight as well, wearing a suit that she had never seen before. His skin looked as if it was glowing. He was walking with a confidence that Stacey hadn't seen on him. It was almost a swagger.

"Well, I don't like it. I'm going to find Charlie to let him know."

She moved away from her sister and headed down one of the hallways. There were numerous rooms here, each holding a few guests. In one, a group was smoking cigars and discussing politics. In another, a woman had her arms draped around a man as he spoke. In the next, was the man that Charlie had been speaking with, but no Charlie.

Stacey walked into the room and politely interrupted the current conversation, asking where Charlie had gone.

The man shrugged a little. "He cut the conversation short. Said he had forgotten something. Looked slightly sick, actually. Are you his wife? I don't know where he went. He left the room in a hurry though. Looked like he was leaving the party."

He turned away from Stacey, clearly not interested in keeping the conversation going. She felt confused by what he had said. Charlie had left? Why in the world would he leave without saying anything? She knew that he had been acting weird all night but to just ditch her at the party…

Her stomach felt as if she had swallowed an entire jar of live butterflies. She left the room and went into the library, closing the door behind her.

Cut off from the buzzing of the party and the fact Tony and Adele were roaming around, Stacey tried calling Charlie. It went right to voicemail. She sighed and looked out the window of the library.

Below was the city, sprawled out like glittering jewels. In the distance, she could see construction in her section of town. She tapped her fingers against the glass, wondering why Charlie had left like that. Was he having second thoughts? Was he –

"Oh, look who it is."

Stacey cursed inwardly and looked over to see Tony as he entered the library. He closed the door behind him and crossed his arms, blocking her only way out.

"Hi, Tony. Follow me in here?"

"Saw you looking for Charlie like a chicken without a head. Sad. Did he get bored already?" His tone was like dry ice. She could see a smirk dancing at the corners of his mouth.

"Are you allowed off your leash this long to talk to me?" Stacey countered.

"Jealousy doesn't suit you, Stacey," he said casually as he ran his fingers along one of the side tables, walking toward her.

"Jealous of what, exactly?"

"Oh, I don't know. That my date is still here, for one. Although, I'm sure Charlie will come back, right? Probably just had to run to the corner store or something," he said mockingly.

Stacey was trying not to get irritated but was quickly failing. She was already nervous about Charlie suddenly leaving. On top of that, to have Tony here, trying to rub it in her face was not something she wanted to deal with.

"Well, this was nice," she remarked, attempting to move past him to leave.

But Tony's hand gripped her arm. She tried to pull back, but he didn't budge. Stacey looked up at him and tried to ignore the fear that was nestling into her stomach.

"I wasn't sure I would see you so soon after you ran away."

"I wasn't running away. I was going home. Let go of me, Tony." She tried to keep her voice stern.

"Don't you see? He has already blown you off, Stacey. You deserve better than that."

"So, what? I deserve a man who has cornered me in this library and refuses to let me leave? The more you act like this, the more I know that I made the right choice."

Tony looked as if she had slapped him. He loosened his grip a little on her arm but still didn't move his hand. Stacey was unnerved by how he was acting. It was weird that he had seemingly gotten this hung up on her.

"I came here with Adele," he said through clenched teeth.

"Not my problem. No one asked you to bring her here. In fact, everyone probably wished that you hadn't."

"I thought… surely, you see now…"

"See what?" Stacey suddenly felt weary from dealing with Tony and his strange moods. "That I wanted you all along? Tony, this needs to stop. I'm flattered that you feel this strongly about me," she lied swiftly, "but we're over. Now let me leave."

He was looming over Stacey now, staring her down as if she was an enemy that needed to fall in line instead of a woman that he loved. In the back of her mind, she realized that she had dodged a bullet by breaking up with him. Stacey backed up until she was pressing against one of the bookshelves.

"Tony. Let me leave this room or I swear I will scream my head off."

"Stacey, you just have to see. You have to understand. I know if I can only make you see that Charlie doesn't care about you. He left you here alone. What sort of man does that? I would never do that to you."

"No, instead you'd trap me in a room and not listen to me when I tell you to let me leave!" she exclaimed loudly, her fear getting the better of her.

She shoved her hands forward and tried to push Tony out of the way. Yet he was like stone. He didn't budge. His grip only tightened on her. She tried to yank her arm free, but she was pressed against the bookshelf.

"We belong together. Adele, she means nothing to me. She is a means to an end."

"Does she know that?"

"She isn't stupid. She knows how I feel about you. Come with me again. We can go anywhere in the world you'd like."

"I'd like to stay here, actually."

Tony brought his face closer to hers. He was going to kiss her, Stacey realized.

"Stacey," he said, and she could feel his breath lightly against her face, "whatever you want, I can give it to you. I love you, Stacey. You're mine."

Stacey tried to wriggle free. The fear in her stomach was real and alive. She opened her mouth to scream in an attempt to get Tony away from her.

But she never got the chance. Tony was suddenly pulled away from her. It was as if a giant magnet had yanked him away. He went falling to the floor. And above him –

"Charlie," Stacey breathed with relief.

Charlie's face was flushed red. His fists were curling and uncurling. Stacey had never seen him look so angry before. Tony scrambled to his feet.

"Don't get the wrong idea, Charlie," Tony said. "She threw herself at me. At me! I was trying to tell her that I was seeing Adele –"

"Are you fucking serious?" Stacey exclaimed, shocked at his lie.

But Charlie was shaking his head. His hands curled up around the collar of Tony's shirt and he slammed him against one of the bookshelves. The bookshelf shook and a few books clattered to the floor. Stacey watched, holding her breath.

"If you come near her again, you're going to regret it," Charlie growled at Tony in a voice she had never heard before.

Stacey went over to him and hovered behind him, finally managing to say, "Charlie, don't."

Charlie's fingers tightened around Tony's collar, holding him in place. Tony said nothing, only letting out a wheezing noise as he stared at Charlie.

He leaned forward and Stacey heard him say, "The only reason I'm not going to kick your ass is because the lady requested that I don't." He released Tony who began to cough. "Try this shit again and I will put an end to you and your entire fucking company."

Before Tony could say anything, Charlie grabbed Stacey's hand. He turned and practically dragged her out of the library. He stalked down the hallway back into the party. Stacey trailed after him as he went up to Jacob and Allison.

"We have to go," he said to them. "It was a lovely party though. Thank you for having us."

Allison looked surprised and glanced over at Stacey who could only shrug. Then she followed Charlie out of the party and into the elevator.

Chapter Fourteen

The elevator ride down was silent except for Charlie's breathing. He didn't look at Stacey. Instead, he was taking slow breaths, holding them and exhaling them after ten seconds. Their fingers were loosely entwined.

She could picture Tony pressed against the bookshelf and Charlie holding onto him. She had been terrified of Tony then. If Charlie hadn't appeared, what would she have done?

Not to mention she was wondering just what Charlie had run off to do. He came back just in time but what if he hadn't?

The elevator doors opened and the two of them left the elevator in silence. They crossed the lobby into the parking lot. For the first time since she had gotten back home, it was actually chilly outside. Charlie must have noticed because he turned to her.

"Want my jacket?"

"No, I'm okay."

He didn't ask again like Tony would have. Like always, Charlie listened to her. Stacey was about to ask where he had gone when Adele came out of the building. When she saw the two of them, she stormed over. Stacey sighed at the same time Charlie did.

"Try not to throttle this one," Stacey joked under her breath. She saw a ghost of a smile cross Charlie's mouth.

"You!" Adele cried, stopping in front of him. "What did you do to Tony?"

"Nothing. He got off easy," Charlie quipped.

"Why don't you ask what your stupid slutty girlfriend tried to do to him?"

Stacey rolled her eyes at the jab. It was tiresome, and Charlie knew there was no way in hell she would have thrown herself at Tony. Charlie's lips were pressed into a thin line.

"Adele," he said patiently, "what the fuck do you want?"

"I want – I want you to apologize to him –"

"Cut the shit," Charlie interrupted. "Listen. Do me a favor, alright? You still talk to my dad and my brother. Tell them I'm done with them. With their plans and everything else they have plotting. It's done."

"What?" Adele laughed. "What does that even mean? What are you going to do?"

Charlie didn't answer. His gaze was steely and for the first time since Stacey had met her, Adele looked unnerved.

"Tell them," he repeated. "And please, get out of my face."

He turned around and walked toward the parking lot. Stacey gave Adele a mocking wave good-bye and followed Charlie. She tried to keep up with his big steps in her high heels. There was no car waiting for them. She didn't know where he was going.

He cut across the parking lot and Stacey could see now that he was heading toward one of the parks.

"Uh, Charlie?" Stacey called out. "I'm wearing four-inch heels. While I appreciate the walk, can we please find a place to sit?"

He stopped walking at the entrance to the park and shook his head. "Sorry, Stacey. Just wanted some fresh air." He held his hand out to her. "Come on."

Stacey took it. Her hand slid comfortably into his. She could feel his heart rate hammering underneath her hand. He was still full of adrenalin and on edge from whatever was bothering him, aside from his confrontation with Tony.

They walked into the park. In the distance, Stacey could hear a band playing. The park had groups of people enjoying the evening together. Charlie took her to a bench nearby in front of the fountain. They sat down together. He was clutching her hand.

"Charlie, mind telling me where you ran off to in the middle of the party?"

"I forgot something."

She waited for him to say more and when he didn't, she cleared her throat. "And you couldn't tell me?"

"No."

"Well, why not?"

Charlie turned to face her. He looked serious now, instead of aggravated. A thought struck Stacey – *Oh God, I'm getting dumped, aren't I?* It would explain a lot of everything going on. Even with that thought, she remained silent.

"Stacey, I have to tell you something."

Her free hand gripped the side of the bench as if to ward off the bad news. "What?"

"I'm taking the money I have and I'm starting a new company."

She blinked, thrown off by the news. It hadn't been what she was expecting at all.

Taking her silence as a sign to keep going, Charlie spoke, "I've been putting a lot of thought into it. I'm sick of letting my family control me. It won't stop unless I do something about it. So, I'm branching off. Starting my own investment firm with the money I've made."

"That's what you meant when you spoke to Adele," Stacey replied.

"That's right. I'm not going to be listening to their shit anymore. I have no interest in it. Stacey, this is going to be a big deal. Leaving my family to try this out is a big risk. It could all blow up. I could end up with no money."

"Is that what you're worried about? Charlie, I don't care if you have no money by the end of this. I'm here no matter what you want to do. If you want to try this, I support you. I don't care about the money."

Charlie smiled at her. He looked slightly more relaxed and stood up.

"Where are we going?"

"Can you walk a little farther? There's someplace I want to show you."

"Sure," Stacey replied, standing.

He took her hand again and led her through the park. She had never been here before. It was beautiful and sprawling. The trees were so tall that sometimes it blocked out the night sky completely.

Around them, couples walked hand-in-hand. There was something nice about being around other people like this. Everyone looked content and happy. They walked together in silence past a small pond. The moonlight reflected in the water and rippled when someone tossed a rock into the pond.

"Ever been to this park?" Charlie asked her at one point.

"Nope. Too far away from my section of the city."

"It's my favorite. If I lived where Jacob did, I'd be down here all the time," he remarked.

She could picture Charlie by the pond, studying it in the daytime. The question was still in her mouth – where had he gone? – but she didn't want to ruin the moment. After another minute of walking, they stopped in front of an older-looking greenhouse. She couldn't see inside of it very well in the dim lighting.

A man stood guard in front of it. It was clearly closed, but Charlie showed him something and the man allowed him through the door.

"Wow, impressive. Didn't realize your name could get us into the hottest greenhouse in town," Stacey joked.

Charlie laughed. The greenhouse had a dome with the stars glittering down on them. He led her through the darkened flowers. The air was heavy with the scent of different flora. It was a nice smell, pleasant and earthy.

When they reached the back of the greenhouse, Stacey gasped. In front of her, small lights had been draped through the leaves. They seemed to perfectly illuminate the roses that were around the back of the greenhouse. It took her breath away. It was simple yet beautiful.

"Do you like it?" Charlie asked her.

"Is this for me?" she asked in surprise.

"No, I normally decorate like this." Charlie laughed at her.

Stacey took a step toward the roses. She liked how each one looked as if they were glowing. She liked the smell of them mixed with the dirt. Above her, the stars twinkled. She felt far removed from the city, as if she were on another planet.

Charlie came up behind her and kissed her gently on the neck. "I'm glad you like it."

"It's gorgeous. But… why?" she asked and turned around to face him. "Is this where you went earlier?"

"Ah, no. I forgot the most important part of this little thing." He gestured around him. "So, I had to go get it."

"Get what?" Stacey asked.

Charlie brought her in for a kiss. There was something different about this kiss. It was soft and gentle, filled with a promise that she didn't quite understand. She returned the kiss and could feel her heart skip a beat.

"Thank you. For stopping Tony. I didn't know –"

"It isn't your fault for anything to do with Tony. He's an asshole. I'm glad I was there. I'm sorry I didn't tell you that I was leaving. I didn't want to spoil the surprise. I wanted it to mean a lot to you and not be mucked up."

"Well… what is the surprise then?" Stacey whispered.

To her shock, Charlie got down on one knee. Her head went light. She swore that she was dreaming this up. But no, Charlie was down on one knee and he pulled out a small box. Her breath caught.

"Stacey, I love you. I've always loved you. And with this new journey ahead of me, I want you to be the one who comes along with me."

She felt the tears spring to her eyes. Her hands felt as if they were trembling. He opened up the ring box. A beautiful diamond ring sat in the center.

"Will you marry me, Stacey?" Charlie whispered nervously.

His nerves made sense. He had somehow forgotten the engagement ring in all of this. That was why he had left. He had to go back and fetch it. Stacey would have laughed if she wasn't crying.

Furiously wiping her eyes, she nodded.

"Yes. Yes, I will marry you."

-To be continued in Book 4-

If you enjoyed this title, I would appreciate your leaving a review of the book. Good reviews encourage an author to write as well as help books to sell. Good reviews can be just a few short sentences describing

what you liked about the book without having a spoiler.
If you could spend 30 seconds writing a review, I
would appreciate it: you can review this title right now
at your favorite retailer.

Here is a preview of the **next book** you may also
enjoy:

Love Confirmed: Persuasive Billionaire BWWM Romance Series, Book 4

EVEN THOUGH it was autumn, the rain was pouring down as if it was one of those summer storms back in the city. The road here wasn't even made out of pavement, but some sort of gravel that stuck to the tires of the car and bounced Stacey around. Her nose was pressed against the passenger side window, as if she could make anything out.

"You alright?" Charlie asked next to her as he slowly rounded a corner.

Stacey cleared her throat. "Nervous."

"You'll be fine. It'll be me that Dad will be flipping his shit over, not you."

He sounded confident, which made sense since it was his father after all. Even so, Stacey couldn't shake the sense of foreboding that was hanging over her. The storm only made her anxiety worse.

"I'm sure you're right," she finally replied, glancing over at him.

The sudden movement made her ring flicker up at her in the dim light. Stacey still wasn't used to seeing it. She wasn't used to what it represented either. She was *engaged* to Charlie. It had been two weeks since their engagement, but it still didn't feel as if it had truly sunk in.

The night that he had decorated the greenhouse and proposed felt like a dream. She clung to the memory now to help her with her nerves. Sure, she had only heard horror stories about Charlie's family. But he was here and would have her back. She had nothing to fear.

"Anyway, just let me handle most of the talking. Dad will be grumpy, but he's always grumpy. He's been that way ever since Mom died," Charlie joked.

His mother. She was one person Charlie had spoken about at length the past couple of weeks. Stacey had never asked him about his mother, mostly because she always sensed that he hadn't wanted to talk about her.

When he finally did, he told her how she had gotten very sick and died when Charlie was eight years old. Eric, his brother, could hardly recall her.

"Dad changed when that happened," Charlie said to her. "It was as if she was the only driving force of good in him. He had always been able to juggle the company and family, but after Mom died… there was no family anymore. Just the company. Always the company."

The words stuck in her head now as they turned onto a larger road. Charlie's father was at their *vacation home* although it was so far out of state and in the country that it wasn't what Stacey pictured when she heard the term. They had been driving for two hours since leaving the airport.

"We're almost there," Charlie said as if reading her mind. "Rain slowed us down a lot."

"Didn't know it rained like this out here."

"Probably just because my dad is in the area." At seeing her face, he cleared his throat. "That was a joke. Sorry. I'm making you more nervous, aren't I?"

"Yes, but I get it. Joking to cope." Stacey smiled weakly.

"One way of putting it," he replied grimly.

Through the front window of the car, Stacey saw it. It was as if it appeared out of nowhere, conjured up by Charlie's joke. Through each wipe of the windshield, she could see a magnificent house before them. It looked more like a manor than just a house.

"Wow," Stacey breathed. "This looks like something I'd picture out of an old novel or something."

"It isn't haunted," Charlie replied, and she looked at him. "What? Don't those old books always have ghosts around the manors? Or the moors. Or something."

"Did you sleep through your fancy English literature class back in college?" she quipped.

Charlie laughed. "Well, it still isn't haunted. Dad just isn't one for being subtle in any occasion. He had this place built after Mom died. Wanted it to look as if it could be dropped down in Scotland and fit right in."

"Well, it definitely looks like that."

They drove through the open iron gates. In the front of the house was a fountain that Stacey could just barely make out through the storm. She looked up to try to see the top of the house. It was decorated with what looked to be gargoyles which only added to the creepy vibe of the place.

Charlie drove around the circular gravel driveway and stopped in front of the manor. The heavy oak doors opened up and two men stepped out. The taller man was holding an umbrella. Together, they walked over to them. One of them opened the back doors of the car and began removing luggage. The other came over to the passenger door and opened it.

"Peter!" Charlie exclaimed, leaning over. "How are you?"

"Good, sir. I've brought an umbrella to escort your fiancée to the front door. Then I can come back to fetch you."

"I'll catch up with you," Charlie said to Stacey.

She nodded and clutched her purse, feeling oddly nervous. She stepped out of the car and was staring at Peter. He was an older-looking man. His hair had gone completely grey and he was slightly hunched over. She reached for the umbrella, but he shook his head once and then turned around to lead her to the front door.

Stacey hurried after him, not wanting to get wet. At the front doors, he ushered her inside. A quick glance showed that the other man was behind her, holding all their luggage. The rain didn't seem to affect him at all. Even so, she felt badly for him.

The door closed behind her and Stacey looked around. They were in what seemed to be an entrance hallway. There was nothing modern about this place. Everything looked old-fashioned as if from an old horror movie set. The hallway was narrow, and the floors were made of hard wood. There was a staircase next to her. Not even one of those spiraling staircases she had been seeing so often lately but a cramped one that reminded her a little of the one on Tony's yacht.

The walls were decorated with paintings, mostly landscapes. The place smelled faintly of mothballs. This was not what Stacey had been expecting. This looked like a place someone who came from old money would live in, not a place that someone would intentionally build.

The front door opened again and Charlie came in. He was soaking wet and holding some of the luggage.

"Sir, I was going to come back for you," Peter said.

"I'm fine, thanks. I didn't want to leave Warren with all the luggage," Charlie replied.

Warren, who looked even older than Peter, smiled a toothy grin. "I'll dry these off and bring them to your rooms."

"Thanks. Wait, uh, rooms?" Charlie asked.

Warren's eyes flicked over to Peter, who spoke up, "Yes, sir. Master Terrence has requested you two sleep in separate rooms since you are not married. It would be improper."

I really have stumbled into some sort of time machine, haven't I? Stacey thought glumly. She looked over at Charlie to see if he was going to say anything. He had said before arriving here that he was going to have to pick his battles, especially with his news. Separate rooms would be weird, but it didn't seem like something to kick a fuss over.

Charlie's lips pressed together in a thin line but he nodded his head in agreement. Stacey relaxed a little. Better not to start things off with a fight about bedrooms. Peter moved past Stacey and began to walk up the stairs.

"This way, please," he said to the two of them without looking back.

Stacey shot Charlie a look but all he did was wiggle his eyebrows in an attempt to make her laugh. They walked up the staircase. The first floor had the same décor as the one below. Paintings along the walls. A carpet that was full of dull colors. The windows were opened, showing the pouring rain outside. All the doors were closed. They stopped at one near the end of the hallway.

"This is your room, sir," Peter said to Charlie, opening it for him.

Stacey peered inside. It was a large room with its own bathroom. The bed was huge and could have easily fit the two of them. There was a couch and a bookshelf on the other wall with a table in front of it.

"Warren will bring your bags up once they're cleaned off, sir."

"Great, thanks. Stacey is going to be next to me?" Charlie asked.

"No, sir. Master Terrence has put Stacey on the fifth floor."

"The fifth floor?" Charlie and Stacey exclaimed in unison.

Peter's face didn't change. All he did was nod. She glanced over at Charlie who looked as if he was about to open his mouth and tell Peter off. Stacey rested her hand on his arm.

"It's fine. It's just a big house, right? Not the end of the world to be on the fifth floor."

"The fifth floor is reserved for guests, ma'am, while these rooms are for family. Nothing personal," Peter said to her.

"Of course. Not a problem. I'll see you later." She directed this to Charlie who still looked furious but nodded in reply.

If you enjoyed this sample then look for **Love Confirmed: Persuasive Billionaire BWWM Romance Series, Book 4**.

Here is a preview of **another story** you may enjoy:

Love Endured: Tenacious Billionaire BWWM Romance Series, Book 3

ADALIA SAT beside the infinity pool at the Grace Hotel and looked out over the deep blue ocean. Trent was inside, a quick business call to sort out his affairs before their honeymoon got into full swing.

She sighed and a smile parted her lips at the taste of salty sea air. Santorini, Greece had been her choice. The quaint white structures and sloping stairs, the city tucked against the mountain, built from the rock itself, was her idea of a fairytale.

They'd arrived a few hours ago and she itched to go out and explore, but there were matters to attend to before they could go anywhere. It irritated her that Trent took the business calls for the bakery, while she didn't have a true business of her own.

One day, she'd be the one in the expensive hotel room, making the calls, buying and selling and checking in on progress. At least, that was her dream.

"You're quiet, my love," Trent said, strolling from the cool interior and taking a seat beside her. He'd opted for an open neck cotton shirt and white pair of slacks. His tan biceps bulged to free themselves from the sleeves restraining them.

Adalia swallowed, overcome by desire again. Every day with Trent was different, an adventure, but one thing would never change – her need for him.

"How was your call?" Adalia asked, squeezing his hand in hers.

"Oh fine, fine. Just some news on the space frontier. We're going live with the IPO in a couple months, so things are going crazy."

"IPO," she repeated, wriggling her eyebrows. "You're opening the company to trade?"

"It's the next big step. We should've done it years ago. Take a look at SkyLyft. They're trading and apart from the debacle with the crash, they're doing pretty damn well." Trent scratched his chin with the tip of his index finger. "But do you really want to talk business, gorgeous?"

"I want to do many things. Including you," she quipped.

He chuckled and picked up a bottle of champagne from the poolside table. He poured for both of them, then handed her one.

"I think we're overdue for a toast after all the shit we've been through," Trent said, then clinked the rim of his glass against hers.

"I couldn't agree more." She raised the flute to her lips. Nausea bubbled in her stomach and she pulled it away again.

"What's wrong?"

"Nothing... I just feel a little strange. I'm fine, really, don't worry." It was probably the plane food.

They'd served some kind of exotic Indian dish and it hadn't gone down well.

Trent slid his arm around her shoulders and pulled her close. He leaned his head against hers and they looked out over the ocean together. "I couldn't have chosen a better destination myself."

"Oh please, you would've had us hiking in Machu Picchu," she said, then pressed a hand to her stomach. Man, the last thing she needed was to start their honeymoon going down on the toilet. That would almost be as bad as DeShawn's attempt to discredit her at the wedding.

Trent's eyes glistened in the morning light. He tipped his head back and soaked up the sun.

Bile crept up Adalia's throat and she stood abruptly.

"What's wrong?" Trent rose immediately and stroked his fingers down her spine.

"I don't know. I just don't feel well." She managed to stand before the nausea completely overwhelmed her. She slapped her palm across her mouth, turned and sprinted for their room. She crashed through into the pristine white suite and grimaced at the off chance she'd let loose before she hit the bathroom.

Adalia skidded around the corner and slid into the bathroom. She didn't have time to close the door. She crouched over the toilet and let breakfast, dinner and what had to be every meal she'd ever eaten present itself in reverse order.

"Oh god, Adalia," Trent hurried into the bathroom and stroked her back. "It's okay, I'm here."

She didn't have the strength to wave him away. So much for romance on their honeymoon. She spent another two minutes in the same state, then flushed the toilet and collapsed against the wall.

Why was everything white in this damn place?

Trent handed her a couple squares of toilet paper and she dabbed at the corners of her mouth. "I'm sorry," she mumbled, "I didn't expect that to happen."

"Don't say sorry, Adalia. It's not like you can help it. I'm worried about you… this looks like food poisoning. We should go see a doctor." He cupped her cheek in his palm and tilted his head to the side, bright blue eyes brimming with concern.

Adalia could barely lift her head. She was exhausted and sweaty, and God, she just wanted a glass of water and a good sleep.

"Don't be ridic –" She pushed him back and vomited noisily into the toilet again. Where could all this have come from –? She'd surely puked out everything else.

"That's it. We're going to see a doctor." Trent rose and hurried into the living room.

Adalia flushed again and struggled into the standing position, then shuffled to the sink. She grasped her cheeks and slapped them to take away the numbness. What the hell was this?

She'd read an article once about eating yogurt to get the local bacteria when visiting a new country, but this was insane. She'd hardly had a chance to unpack. Hell, she'd eaten nothing since they'd arrived, not even a sip of damned champagne.

Adalia brushed her teeth, then washed her mouth out and gargled. That would have to do for now – there was no helping the clammy hands and weak knees.

Trent appeared in the doorway. "Are you done?"

"Yeah, I'm okay. Trent, we really don't need to go to the doctor. It's just a bug… it will pass."

"Like hell it will. Let's go. There's a doctor just around the corner." He guided her from the bathroom with a smile and a gentle caress in the small of her back.

If you enjoyed this sample then look for **Love Endured: Tenacious Billionaire BWWM Romance Series, Book 3**.

Here is a preview of **another story** you may enjoy:

Loved Requited: Ardent Billionaire Romance Series, Book 3

"**I'M SO** proud of you Deirdre. Here's to a successful demo recording." Cassie smiled. Deirdre lifted her glass of champagne to her friend's toast.

"Brooke said it went really well," Deirdre told her friend. "She said we can expect a decision from the studio execs in the next week or so." Deirdre had spent all day recording what could turn into her first album. She'd been working for weeks, choosing songs that were perfectly suited for her strong soprano voice. This after recording dinner with Cassie was the first time she'd allowed herself to relax in six weeks.

"I just know they're going to sign you. You deserve something fantastic like this, Dee." Cassie smiled. "And just think of all of the things you'll be able to do for D'Angelo. You're going to be able to give him an amazing life."

An uncomfortable look spread across Deirdre's face. "Do you really think so? Felix is afraid that if I'm in the public eye, D'Angelo will suffer for it… I'm afraid he has a point. I mean, look at how most celebrity kids turn out. It's ridiculous… I'd never want that for my brother. I loved recording the demo, but maybe this isn't something I should pursue. Maybe I should just keep focusing on school and let D'Angelo have a quiet life." Deirdre sighed.

Cassie took a long sip of her champagne and studied her friend. "Do you really think that a little attention and money will be worse for D'Angelo than what he's already been through?" she asked firmly. Deirdre opened her mouth to respond, but Cassie kept plowing on. "He deserves the best, even more than you do. And you're a good person, Dee. You'll make sure he is too." She paused for another moment before continuing. "This doesn't sound like you, Deirdre. Whose idea was it for you to turn down the deal?"

Deirdre looked down before answering. "Felix just pointed out that fame can be fleeting. And leave lasting damage. I just don't know what the right thing is…"

"And Parker? I'm assuming you're still talking to him?" Cassie prodded.

Deirdre shook her head. "He's been keeping his distance. He sent flowers once… he's sent over food with notes, saying he's thinking about me, knows I'm busy. And he's been taking D'Angelo to ball games… but he always stays in the hallway… like he's literally giving me my space. He said he'd wait as long as it takes, I'm starting to think he meant it."

"Maybe I misjudged our handsome billionaire," Cassie conceded. "And maybe you should talk to him about your decision. Who would know better about the pros and cons of having enormous loads of money?" She laughed.

"I'd love to talk to him about this," Deirdre agreed, "but I'm not sure I can trust myself around Parker. The last time we were alone together, I almost cheated on Felix. He doesn't deserve that."

"Deirdre, it almost sounds like you're staying with Felix out of obligation. Aren't you the one who pointed out that he deserves better than that?" Cassie reminded her.

Deirdre sighed. "And aren't you the one who said I was allowed to take time?" She countered.

"Yes… but that was back when Felix seemed like a good fit for you. The longer you've stayed with him, the less I think that. He's discouraging you from taking advantage of a once in a lifetime opportunity… It almost sounds like he's intimidated by the idea of you succeeding."

"Felix loves D'Angelo,'" Deirdre snapped defensively. "He's just trying to make sure I put his needs first, that's all. You should see the two of them together, Cass. D'Angelo loves him. And Felix has a point; my decisions affect my brother as much as they affect me."

"It sounds like Felix wants you to put HIS needs first and he's hiding behind an eight year old," Cassie said firmly. She sighed. "We've gotten off track, Dee, tonight was supposed to be a celebration. Take the deal or don't take the deal, it doesn't change the fact that this is a pretty big honor. I'm proud of you." Cassie smiled.

"It is kinda a big honor, isn't it?" Deirdre smiled, allowing her friend to change the subject.

Cassie nodded. "And it could be the beginning of the rest of your life."

If you enjoyed this sample then look for **Loved Requited - Ardent Billionaire Romance Series, Book 3.**

Other Books by Shyla Starr

- Tenacious Billionaire BWWM Romance Series

- Elusive Billionaire Romance Series

- Lonely Billionaire Romance Series

- Ardent Billionaire Romance Series

- Fervent Billionaire BWWM Romance Series

- Audacious Billionaire BWWM Romance Series

Get the latest update on new releases from the author at:

https://shylastarr.com/newsletter/

About the Author - Shyla Starr

Shyla currently specializes in writing interracial romance stories and is a huge fan of the alpha male. Simply put, there just aren't enough stories about mixed couple romances, which is something she is aiming to fix.

Being a bookworm all her life, when Shyla discovered men she also realized how easy it was to fulfill her fantasies through her writing.

When not writing and fantasizing about men, Shyla enjoys dancing, reading and chilling with her friends.

Connect with Shyla Starr

I really appreciate you reading my book! Here are my social media coordinates:

Friend me on Facebook: https://www.facebook.com/shylastarrauthor

Follow me on Twitter: https://twitter.com/shylstarr

Check me out on Goodreads: https://www.goodreads.com/author/show/8436084.Shyla_Starr

Subscribe to my newsletter: https://shylastarr.com/newsletter/

Visit my website: https://shylastarr.com/

9 781773 500577